OUTSIDE THE BIG OAK DOORS

Fiction

BY MICHELLE TOCHER

TABLE OF CONTENTS

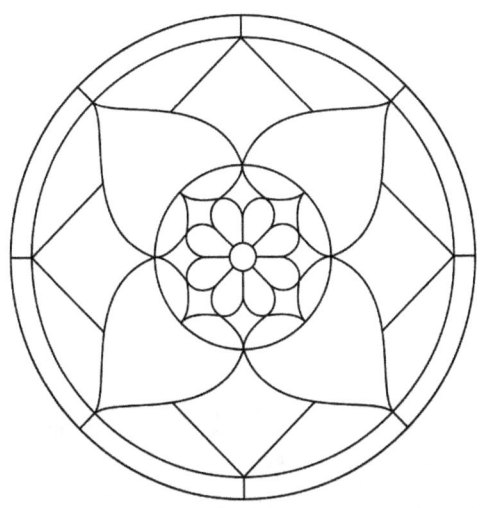

CHAPTER 1

CHARLIE'S HALO

Whenever the fighting got real bad, we'd explode into our separate rooms and then Mama would come to our doors, poke her head in and say, "Try to understand Charlie. He's got the gift of faith."

Of the four of us, Charlie was the special one. Mama always gave him shelter in the heat, and if that failed, well then, there was always God. He was Mama's chief minion, and his best defense was to make a scene just at the point when you knew she'd come hollering, sweep us out of the room like bats, and stay after with Charlie, who'd weep like Jesus.

Charlie's halo grew with his shoe size, and by the time he was eight he was singing solos in the church choir in his tiny, plaintive voice, and starting rows so memorable I could snatch a dozen from my memory at the click of a switch. I didn't dislike Charlie. We usually ended up laughing over the boneheaded things he did. But Aunt Bel detested him.

Mama's older sister Isabel lived with us for a few years after we first came to Calgary in 1962, but even before that, when we lived in Toronto, she was always in the picture. At Christmas, Bel would buy us wonderful, impractical things like trucks and trains and dolls with boobs. But Charlie would get socks. Socks that went to mid calf and slid down from there, so he always looked goofy in a pair of shorts and running shoes. Charlie didn't mind, though. Before he started junior high, he was as comical as a clown, with a little pot belly that couldn't hold up his hand-me-downs. Mama took to strapping him in suspenders once he got old enough to blush when adults sniggered at his bare half moon. Charlie could put us in stitches like no one else on the block, just by showing up. When he had a story to tell, we laughed so hard we burst our buttons. Even Bel would smirk. I don't ever recall her snorting, though, which is what she would do if something was "too funny", as she put it.

Bel gave Charlie credit for a diabolical intelligence in proportion to the size of his halo. She used to counter Mama's gift-of-faith line by pulling us aside and whispering, "I know he started it. I saw him engineer the whole thing." My eyes would pop. I marveled at Charlie's power to manipulate situations and know who would come out accused at the other end. For me, it only confirmed the notion that he had connections in high places.

One night, one of Jeffrey's records went missing—a forty-five by the Rooftop Singers called *Walk Right In.* Jeffrey tore the house apart in a bulldog rage and got into a big fight with Mama, who lined us up in the living room and demanded to know whodunnit. Nobody fessed up. Eight-year-old Zack, the youngest of my brothers, got accused because he didn't have an alibi, and also because everybody knew he loved to listen to Jeffrey's music. Zack got sent to the room he shared with Charlie. While he was there, he rifled through Charlie's stuff and found the record under his pillow. He took it straight to Mama, who took Charlie by the scruff of the neck and steered him to her room. She shut the door and spoke softly, while Charlie wept. When she came out, she said Charlie had just wanted to learn the song. He was in the choir, after all, and he needed to practice his singing. Jeffrey shouted, "What a load of bullshit!" Then he took Zack out to the backyard to throw a football "and pretend it's Charlie's head," Zack said under his breath as they trooped past me.

Later that night, I heard Bel tiptoe down the hall to the boys' bedroom. Naturally I wasn't going to let the opportunity slip, so I followed her and watched their reflections in the mirror over the dresser. Charlie was trying to pull his head through the neck of his new flannelette pajama top, when Bel whipped it away from him and launched into something that made me so mad I nearly lost my cover.

She loomed over him, her hair all wrapped up in rollers and her big breasts cinched into a red silk dressing gown embroidered with dragons. "I've been watching you, young man," she said, "and I know exactly what you're up to."

"You do?" Charlie hugged his bare chest and shivered. He looked like a skinny cherub with his curly blond hair and his wide-open eyes.

Bel crossed her arms over her bosom as if she were God's own judge. "You're doing the devil's work. And don't you dare tell me I don't know what I'm talking about, because I know a whole lot more about life than some puny kid."

Charlie's face went beet red. Bel took a seat next to him on the bed, holding her spine straight and keeping herself a safe distance away from his diabolical influence. "I've seen your kind of troublemaking before. You need sharp eyes to spot the devil's schemes because you folks can be tricky." She nailed him with her iron glare. "You understand what I mean?"

"No, Aunt Bel. Honest, I don't."

"There are powerful forces battling over the fate of our souls, right here in this very room. Some souls get taken for good purposes and others get taken for evil ones, and there isn't much we can do about it."

"Are you sayin' I've been taken by the devil?" It looked like Charlie was about to bolt and tell Mama that Aunt Bel had said he'd been taken by the devil. But Bel grabbed his arm and kept him pinned to the bed. "You know exactly what I'm saying."

"I don't mean to make trouble," Charlie whimpered.

"Oh, yes you do."

She yanked his arm to make her point, and then she let him go. "Anyway, your powers are still pretty unsophisticated. It'll be some time before you can start wars or spread plagues and famines. You might be able to keep the devil in check. But let me tell you, what your mother calls your 'gift of faith' is a terrible curse." She shook her long forefinger at him. "You think your halo protects you, but the fact of the matter is, devils hide behind halos."

Satisfied with her sermon, Bel stood up to go.

Charlie was trembling all over. "How am I gonna keep the devil in check?"

"Well, you'll have to fight it, and fight it hard. The road to hell is paved with good intentions." Bel tossed him his pajama shirt and then I ducked into the bathroom because she was headed for the door.

When she'd disappeared along the hall and I could hear her slippers flapping down the stairs, I rushed into the room. Charlie was sitting frozen on his bed, clutching his pajama top.

"Christ!" I cried. "You don't believe her, do you?"

He looked up at me coolly and narrowed his eyes. "I'm not Christ, Alice. I'm the Antichrist."

"You wanna know what you are? You're an idiot," I said. And I left.

I did a lot of serious thinking about Charlie at that

time. He had been born prematurely, and I figured if he'd just had that extra month, he wouldn't have wasted so much time trying to crawl back into the womb. He didn't make many friends. In the summers he spent most of his time alone in the park. He liked all kinds of animals, even insects, and he would trap them in shoeboxes or bottles. Then he'd bring them home so he could look them up in the *Encyclopedia Britannica*. Once he'd written the information down in his book, he would set the creature free.

Lots of times I felt sorry for Charlie. But you had to be careful about that. One day I snatched his animal book and ridiculed him because he had given the name Margery to a leaf beetle. "Is Margery your girlfriend?" I teased. We were in the backyard, and I'd gone to sit on the swing. Charlie's face turned as red as the bug's shell, and I felt guilty. I got to my feet to hand him the book, and he took a swing at me. Punched me so hard in the face, I thought he'd broken my jaw. Right when I started to feel sorry for him, that's when he spied his opportunity, and the force of that punch wasn't like anything on earth, and I hope not like anything beyond it, either.

A year or two after Bel fed him that line about being the devil, Charlie started doing some pretty strange things. He quit the church choir and joined a gang of punks who hung out down by the ravine. He wouldn't let anyone cut his wild hair, and he lost his sense of humor completely, except when he was with those curs who giggled enough to give you the creeps. We didn't have any more arguments, at least not ones that brought the house down. He buddied up with this one guy who smelled like a dead carp and liked to blow things up, especially mailboxes, so I guess that's how Charlie got it out of his system.

The juvenile delinquency carried on until just before Charlie entered high school, and then he did another flip flop. Suddenly, and for no apparent reason, he beat a retreat from his creepy friends and took to staying at home and reading Mama's Bible. It was a heavy, leatherbound book that scared off the rest of us. We'd either break our backs trying to lift it, or risk tearing one of its delicate, gold-trimmed pages. Mama kept it on a stand in the living room, like a shrine to Grampa, and I don't know if Charlie got permission to take it, or if he just hauled it away, but Mama didn't seem to mind its disappearance.

To begin with, Charlie locked himself downstairs in the rec room after school and on weekends. Sometimes you could hear him sobbing down there, but no one ventured to intrude. One evening when Charlie was fifteen, he came upstairs for dinner with his hair all messed up and scratches on his forehead as if he'd been wearing a crown of thorns. Mama said, "Charlie, are you all right?" He nodded, bowed his head, and whispered prayers into his steepled hands. Mama passed him a plate of shepherd's pie. "Come on now, Charlie, leave your flock for a minute and have something to eat." Charlie pushed it away with the tip of a finger. You'd think the food had been poisoned. "He's the Lord's Shepherd, he shall not want lamb," Jeffrey said. "Here, give it to me." He pulled it over to his side of the table. At twenty, Jeffrey had started university and grown his red-brown hair to his shoulders. His jaw was covered in a rusty bristle that made him look like a rock star. He shoveled the food into his mouth and sputtered, "Sweet lamb of God, that's delicious."

Mama laid a hand on Jeffrey's arm to shush him and slid Charlie a basket of bread rolls. He didn't say "thank you." During those days, he rarely answered when he was spoken to. I don't remember anyone ever telling him to sit up straight or get his elbows off the table because, as Mama said, "Charlie's got the gift of faith."

I know Mama worried that Charlie's new fanaticism might be more dangerous than his delinquency, but she tried to shrug it off, hoping that when Charlie emerged from heaven and hell, he'd come out somewhere in the middle. Instead, daily life got more complicated because when he reached sixteen, Charlie started opening his mouth again. The sermons were unbelievable. He carried a portable Bible under his arm, and we got more sermons from him than we'd ever had from Mama or the priests. So, we all despised him and left him alone.

After a while, he got involved with some Baptists and trooped off to worship with them. I'll never forgive him for trying to spoon-feed me St. Paul and all that crap about paternal authority and how women belong in the back pews while their menfolk go about uncoiling the Truth. The only thing that saved me from detesting him was he had found a girlfriend, a dour Baptist girl who wore an assortment of small crocheted doilies on her head. Making fun of her provided us with hours of entertainment.

Mama was Charlie's only real support during this period, and even she started wondering where she went wrong when it became clear that his fervor was getting pathological. I think she figured he would become a priest, but he didn't want that. He wanted to do Christ's work in the "real world" where the truly scummy souls were to be found. Better to clean a filthy floor than a dirty one. Now I could understand that.

But it was only a pipe dream he had about joining this or that, and going to faraway places where he could feed bloated bellies with the body and blood of Christ. Instead he just continued going to school like everybody else, while choosing to ignore anything that didn't fit neatly into God's handiwork. Which, for starters, meant that he snubbed us all.

His halo seemed to harden around him. It was as if he built himself an unassailable fortress that no one could enter, and after a while, nobody tried. We still laughed at him, but he wasn't funny. It was the only way we knew how to react without revealing how much we despised him. Maybe Charlie sensed our scorn because he recoiled and drifted away.

In 1973, just after Charlie turned eighteen, Mama went off to Grampa's funeral. Bel reappeared, offering to supervise the household in lieu of attending the service. We didn't need supervision, especially hers, but Mama deferred, if only to assuage Bel's guilt feelings. Bel had been adopted when she was eight years old, and while she claimed Grandma as her exclusive property, she never had a strong attachment to Grampa.

On the morning of the funeral, I found Bel sitting at the kitchen table in a green silk housecoat, flipping through the newspaper, and smoking, which was not allowed in the house.

I went to the cupboard to get a juice glass. "Do you wish you were at Grampa's funeral right now?" I asked.

"Heavens no. I've already buried one father, I don't need to bury two," she said, snapping the paper.

All I knew about Bel's father is that he had sent her mother to the Institute for the Feeble Minded in Edmonton in 1927 because she had contracted a disease. A year later, young Isabel was packed onto a train and sent to Cobourg, Ontario to live with her mother's sister Mabel and her husband Gerald Duval.

"How long ago did your father die?" I asked, reaching into the fridge for a jug of raspberry Kool-Aid.

"Three years after my mother was institutionalized." She lowered the paper to her lap and blew a long stream of smoke up to the ceiling.

"Oh yeah?" I concentrated on pouring my drink. I didn't want to turn this into a big conversation.

"He died of a stroke, if you must know," she said, stubbing out her cigarette. "I don't think he could bear the sight of her. Who could? She had the sleepy sickness, you know." She sniffed. "Ever seen anyone with *encephalitis lethargica*?"

"No."

"She looked like this." Bel stiffened her body and twisted it into a hideous shape. The newspaper slid to the floor. She screwed her jaw to one side and raised her arms up into the air with her hands clawed, as if they were about to attack. By the time she came out of her pose, I had fled in terror.

During the time that Bel was "supervising" us, Charlie, true to character, tried to win her affection. I guess he figured he had to do penance for earlier sins that everyone, except Bel, had forgotten. Maybe he never got past believing what Bel had said and wanted to show her that things were different now.

He slaved around the house, outside and inside, from dawn to dusk, cutting, trimming, repairing, wiping down, and putting everything in order. He labored for a whole week until there was nothing left for Bel to attack. I felt terrible for him because it was so obviously futile. Bel would never acknowledge his halo.

Then finally, toward the week's end, she gave him a few dry chaffs of praise. I can still see Charlie standing there in the kitchen, leaning on the sink with the late afternoon sun on his straw hair and his ears flushed pink. Bel crossed her arms under her heavy bosom and said, "You know, Charlie, you really do work hard." He grinned and knitted his fingers together, stretching his arms out uncomfortably. Bel opened the refrigerator and pulled out a carton of milk. Then, in an offhand way, she said, "But what I can't understand, dear, is why you don't just go out like everyone else and make some friends. You don't have any *friends*."

Charlie went out into the crew-cut backyard and crouched against a pole of the swing set we had long outgrown. I watched him from the kitchen window, and I knew he was crying under the fists he held over his head. Bel went around the table, laying out the placemats, and didn't once look out the window to see the damage she had done.

I ran out the door to see what I could do for Charlie. The whole thing was so pathetic. I just wanted to hold him and tell him to forget her. She wasn't worth it anyway.

I knelt beside him and placed my hand on the soft red flannel of his lumberjack shirt. I could feel the hard muscle underneath.

"Go away, Alice," he said.

"But Charlie—"

"Get lost!" he screamed in a high and broken voice.

"Okay, okay," I said, standing up. I figured Charlie was too embarrassed to let me in, but then again, he always did have to work things out his own way. He just wouldn't let go of his cross. He never confided in anyone, not even Mama. I think he was afraid. Afraid of entering the ordinary world, of giving up his halo, and disappearing into the heathen crowd.

After he got out of his teens, Charlie let the halo go. I don't know how it happened. Maybe it got zapped in some big cosmic revelation. Or maybe he wore it askew for a while and then it slipped off when he wasn't looking. All I know is that Charlie can make me laugh again. Really cry. And that's saved everything. Aunt Bel be damned.

CHAPTER 2

UNDER THE RUG

I always got the inside jobs. Now I admit, I loathed yanking a rake through the grass and pushing a shovel, especially after Arctic winds had frozen the ground. But if there was a land of opportunity to be had, it most certainly wasn't to be found between a grimy sink and a toilet. There was nothing romantic about being the only girl in a pack of brothers who get into the snowblowing business early on, and divide the lawn up into strips to be mowed between innings. The job always got done, the games never stopped, and they always came out the winners.

Not to complain. There were certain advantages to the arrangement. I was in charge of all the indoor activities and usually heard the inside story months before the boys caught on. I learned a lot about how crazy people really are, especially grown-ups. They seemed so levelheaded when they were giving us advice, but I never saw a cow pie that they didn't go out of their way to step into. Consequently, I found myself a whole storehouse of inside entertainment and sometimes I even forgot there was an outside world. I can say with pride that I soon became a walking encyclopedia of family trivia, and buried in those tomes were a few steamy scandals that required not a little patchwork and some late-night shifts.

Knowing my penchant for secrets, my brothers usually didn't want me tagging along, and if I did get invited to join them, it was a sure sign that things were going to drag. On a few occasions, however, they had ulterior motives. One day, they invited me to try out the rope swing they had looped over a limb of the old willow in the ravine. It was the fall of 1963, the year after we had moved to Calgary. I was sitting up hill on a lookout platform we had made in an old maple.

"Hey, Alice!" Jeffrey shouted. "Come on down and try this out!"

I scrambled down the tree, jumped to the ground, and ran over to where they stood. A fat rope dangled over the stream.

"What do you want me to do?"

Jeffrey slid down the muddy embankment and reached over the creek to grab the rope. "All you have to do is hold on tight," he said, climbing back up. "Grip it like this." He demonstrated, cinching his fists around the rope and yanking it taut.

"Will it hold me?"

"Sure, it will!" Charlie shrilled. "C'mon, Alice, you're braver than all the rest of us put together."

Zack's shrewd eyes were blazing. He was only seven, but he knew something was wrong with this picture.

Not me. I scrambled up the willow, took the rope from Jeffrey, and gripped it tight, just like he said. I came flying out of that tree like Jane, landed in the stream like a hippo, and couldn't even retaliate because I had to keep my fists stretched flat for weeks so the scabs wouldn't crack. After that I decided they could have their outdoor games. They were just playing in the dirt—and dirt was pretty foul anyway, full of things I wouldn't pick up with my shoe.

I took to my lot with new conviction, combed the house for its litter of gossip, which I scribbled in my diary, cultivated the art of what Bel called "precocious inquiry", and read a lot of books. Mama was working two part-time jobs, which amounted to overtime. Bel would drive her to the office in south Calgary, where she did secretarial work for an advertising firm on 17th Street. Then Mama would turn around and bus it to a real estate agency where she answered phones from four until six. Bel had a bad back, or so she claimed, so I did most of the housecleaning. I tried to avoid her as much as possible, but I spied on her a lot because, of all the people I knew, Bel was the most enigmatic. One look under her rug and you were likely to find the whole city dump.

I was given to understand that from the time they were little, Mama and Isabel had had a conflicted relationship. Grandma Duval was a fervent Anglican who came to Canada from Yorkshire, England, and Grampa Duval was a French-Canadian Catholic who preferred to stay that way. He had a quiet nature, a sweet whispering voice and a gentle presence.

The Christmas after Zack was born in 1956, Grandma and Grampa came to visit us in Toronto. Grampa would rock the baby for hours and sing him French-Canadian songs that could lull anybody to sleep. Zack was a fragile baby, and Grampa would wrap him up in a yellow crocheted blanket, along with Dolly, a soft little crocheted doll that seemed to have been born with Zack. I was four at the time, and I loved listening to Grampa singing. I sat so long at the foot of his rocker that Mama called me "*sa douce petite chienne*" or "his sweet little dog".

Grampa went to church every Sunday, but he didn't force his religion on anybody. He let Grandma take over in matters pertaining to religion and the running of the house. Mama was only two when Isabel joined the family, and from the time she made her appearance, she claimed Grandma as her own mother. Every Sunday, Isabel went with Grandma to the Anglican Church, and I can just imagine how she wedged herself in between Madeline and her Mama. Madeline soon decided that she wanted to go with *her* Papa to *his* church, and from then on, the competition between the two girls became downright hostile.

The battle was only aggravated by the fact that Mama was stunning. I remember an old black-and-white picture of Madeline standing in front of the pavilion on the Cobourg beach. She was somewhere in her teens, and the ribbons in her long auburn hair were fluttering in the breezes flying off the lake. The wind had set out to peek under her floral swing-dancing skirt and she was holding it down, laughing, and showing her perfect teeth. Bel wasn't in the photograph. She never liked having her picture taken. "They don't do me justice," she would say.

In the pictures of Bel that do exist, she had straight brown hair in a style that didn't change all through her twenties and thirties. It was lopped off at the earlobes and snipped unevenly over her brows. She had a sensual mouth, a pretty smile, but a perfectly disastrous nose. She never learned to joke about it either, and insisted on wearing big wide-brimmed hats to cover it. The result was that all you ever saw in the photographs was her nose, sticking out like a peninsula from the uncharted shadows of her face. It was probably unfair that Mama got more attention, but from all reports she was Grandpa's darling, and maybe Grandma's too, even though it was Bel who queued up behind Grandma for communion at the Anglican Church.

In their early teens Bel despised Madeline and went out of her way to make trouble for her. Mama had a pretty voice, and one day when Grampa's brother Gene came to visit, he taught Madeline to sing *"J'addendrai"* ("I Will

Wait"). She was a budding thirteen-year-old and they sat together at the piano while Grandma and Grampa listened in rapture. Then Bel burst into the living room and flounced on the Chesterfield between them. She couldn't stop fidgeting and every time Madeline hit a high note, she cried "ouch!" When Mama's voice began to waver, Bel got to her feet and headed out of the room waving her hands over her head like she was fighting a hive of wasps. "I'll tell you who can't wait. I can't wait for this to stop!"

Madeline had trouble holding her own, and by her seventeenth year, she had quit singing altogether. She went to study art in Toronto, and that's where she met Papa. One night when she was late for her evening class at The Grange, she flagged down a taxi instead of taking a streetcar. I imagine it being one of those muggy early spring nights that get you all agitated and make you wish you lived in a paperback novel. The man behind the wheel—Jonathan Jacob Montgomery—had already been a cabbie for four or five years, and before that he'd been stationed on the east coast. During the Second World War, he was conscripted, but he refused to go active. He became what people called "a zombie". He never said much about those times, only that his father had disinherited him for being a pacifist. In 1944, when it looked like even the zombies were going to get sent overseas, Papa left his station on the east coast, hitched a ride to Montreal, and started to drive a taxi. Eventually, he returned to Toronto, where he continued to drive a cab. He never received a penny from his father, although the old man was a real estate developer with "pockets full of gold", as Papa would say.

Papa didn't care much about appearances. When he picked Mama up that first evening, he hadn't combed his curly brown hair and his face was covered in a week's growth. Still, there was something about him that distracted Madeline, and after a few blocks she realized what it was. His eyes. That's all she could see in the rearview mirror. And did Papa ever have eyes. They were deep-set and blue as the evening sky, and they smiled through you as though they shared all your secret thoughts. He could capture a mermaid with those eyes, and that's how he captured Mama, right there in the rearview mirror.

She forgot the scruffy hair and the stubble. By the sound of it, she even forgot where she was headed. She was so distracted by his eyes that she probably glanced at them a thousand times in the space of a couple of blocks. According to Mama, they didn't exchange many words, but there must have been an intense electric current running through that cab, because when Mama got out, Papa asked her if he could come by to see her artwork. She said "yes", and that's where the story got edited.

What we did know was that when Papa saw Mama's dancing sculptures, he was enthralled. They were lean, energetic figures made out of wire and wax. According to the story, he asked her, "Do you have any idea what these dancers are worth?" She laughed and said, "The moon and the stars?" He kissed her and told her to never sell them for less.

When we were little, Papa would sometimes repeat those lines, especially if we were whining about Mama being locked upstairs on the third floor in her art studio. She often worked while we ate dinner. She'd prepare the meal, pour herself a Scotch and soda, ring the dinner bell, and fly away.

"What's Mama doing up there that's so important?" Jeffrey asked one night when Papa had taken the casserole out of the oven, and we were gathering around the dining room table. Jeffrey was mad because it was the day before Hallowe'en, and he'd made a robot costume that he wanted to show her. The getup was what you would expect from a fourth-grader, just a cardboard box turned upside down with a hole cut in the top and some buttons and squares drawn on with a black marker. He'd already shown it to Bel who had come for a visit, and to Papa, but it was Mama's approval he wanted.

Papa took our plates and scooped chicken and mashed potatoes onto each one in turn. "She's painting, Jeffrey, and you know that's important."

"How important?" Charlie piped, taking his plate.

"More important than the moon and the stars," said Papa.

"More important than me?" Charlie screeched.

"More important than all of us."

Papa's statement had a silencing effect, punctuated by Bel, who simply huffed, "*Well.*"

I'm sure Mama was enchanted by the prospect of being so completely adored by Papa, although he said he put a lot of effort into getting her to say "yes". Once his heart had found its home, he focused everything on her happiness. Over the four-year period before they were married, he quit driving a cab, got a job at a bank, rose to the position of loan manager, converted to Catholicism, and emerged from it all a bright and shiny, brand newly married man.

Throughout my early childhood, the climate in our house swung from the tropics to the poles with not much in between. Sometimes, the cold wars went on for months. But then so did the heat waves. And those were high times for all of us.

Papa died of a heart attack in the spring of 1962. He was only forty-two. His first attack came in November of the year before, but he recovered and went back to work. Then, out of the blue, he had the second attack that killed him. Shortly afterwards, Bel persuaded Mama to move us all from Toronto to Calgary where she lived. She offered to help out until Madeline got back on her feet. At that point Mama had been driven nearly round the bend with worry over finances and schooling, so she agreed. We moved in 1962, at the end of July. Jeffrey was twelve, I was ten, Charlie was seven, and Zack had just turned six.

I was appalled. All I'd ever seen of Bel forced me to conclude that she was a very unpleasant character, to say the least. I begged Mama not to uproot us. I told her I would stay home forever and look after the kids—anything to avoid living with the Wicked Witch of the West. Mama just smiled at me knowingly and said that Bel had changed. "You'll see," she said.

We arrived at the baggage claim in the Calgary Airport, crumpled as wet laundry, all tired and edgy. Mama could hardly manage to haul the bags off the carousel, so Jeffrey did the heavy lifting. Her curly hair was messily tied back, her cheeks were drawn, and she looked as if any minute she'd topple over. We waited in the corner of the baggage area like a group of refugees. Bel was half an hour late before she made her entrance. Wearing a brown velour vest to cover her bulging bosom and tummy, she came flapping towards us like Mother Goose bringing in her gaggle.

Bel gave Mama a big hug and then stood back and looked at her sister shivering in an emerald green cardigan. "Goodness gracious, Madeline, look how thin you are. You're hardly even *here*!" She swept her under her wing. "Not to worry. We'll get you fattened up soon enough." Waving her arms to bring us into her sphere, she clucked, "Come along, my dears, bring your things. Let's get this show on the road!"

We followed her down the corridor to the doors leading out to the taxi cabs. I held Zack's hand, but he started pulling away when he saw how much space he could run into. He dropped Dolly, his crocheted rag doll, and when I bent to pick it up, he bolted. Everybody else had gone outside, and Bel, who was holding the door, slapped a big hand on Zack's arm as he scrambled by. "We'll have to keep this one on a tight leash," she said in a husky voice. I stuffed Dolly into my shoulder bag, took Zack's hand, and steered him out to the cars that were waiting. He fought me, shrieking, "I don't want to go!"

"I know, I know, kiddo," was all I could say.

Bel had found us a good-sized house to rent in the south end of the city. We didn't have any furniture because Mama sold it all out east, but the house was partly furnished, and Bel made up the difference with her stuff. It was all cheap veneered junk with metal legs and shiny surfaces, but it was a whole lot better than nothing.

The boys seemed to like the place because there was so much parkland nearby to be explored. They could disappear into the ravine for hours, where no one could drag them out with a weekend's list of chores. I made some discoveries of my own. One was that Bel had a man friend by the name of Roland. For the longest time, I never saw him, and frankly I don't know much about the nature of Bel's relationship with him. She always went out to see him—never brought him home—and only rarely stayed overnight with him.

One day, shortly after our first experience with an Albertan blizzard, I heard Bel talking to Roland on the phone in her bedroom on the other side of the hall. I was cleaning the bathroom floor for Mama, who had to share that bathroom with Charlie and Zack.

At first, their conversation was just full of the usual meaningless babble. Then there was a long silence at her end, and I heard her shut the door. I jumped up and went out into the hall. I tiptoed around to the other side of the gallery and pressed my ear to her bedroom door.

"No," I heard her say. "Things seem fine. Well, you know, fine as they can be, given the circumstances."

There was a momentary pause while Bel listened.

"Well, I had to tell her. I couldn't *not* tell her, Ro. Jon's been dead now for nearly a year....

"No, she's gone out for a walk. Of course, she's upset. Oh dear, it's all really too bad, isn't it? Poor dear, too bad."

Another pause.

"Well, you're right about that, and I don't imagine we'll hear any more about it. But it'll take a while, these things do, and she's been through her share. But what else could I do? If I'd kept that letter under my hat any longer, she'd think I'd deceived her."

Then she lowered her voice so it was barely audible. "Zack will never know, and I'm sure the kids won't either. But it'll probably come out soon enough that he was adopted. I mean, Maddy's got to say something."

Now *this* was a scoop. Why hadn't we caught on to

it before? You'd think Jeffrey, being six at the time Zack was born, would have suspected something. I don't remember anything. Zack just arrived, like all the rest of us. Obviously, Mama knew, but she'd never so much as hinted. It was too unbelievable.

"I'm sorry I ever got drawn into the middle of this mess, Ro. I really am. But you can't ignore the instructions of a dying man. It's just too much. Too much."

What was she talking about? A letter from Papa? It had to be. But why would he write *her* a letter?

Letters between our family and Bel were infrequent at the best of times. She would come east maybe twice a year and stop by for a week or two en route to Cobourg, where Grandma and Grampa lived. She taught elementary school in Calgary, and so she was free during the summers, but we didn't know what she was up to most of the time. When she did visit, Mama would be a nervous wreck—everything had to be just right for Isabel. Bel had a critical eye, and when she'd glare at you from across the table for some small thing, like cramming too much food into your mouth, you'd gag on your mashed potatoes until you wanted to puke. Every time you did something wrong, she'd peck at you like a crow, and Mama's chin would quiver and twitch until you could see the tears welling underneath her eyelids. Papa knew how flustered Mama could get around her sister, and he would often cut Bel off before she launched into something he knew would be hurtful.

Bel would comply. She always deferred to Papa. They seemed to have some kind of understanding, but I knew, in no uncertain terms, that it was not at all in character for Papa to write Bel letters of any kind.

I couldn't get any more from the telephone conversation, because by this time Bel was whispering. I wasn't even sure if she'd put the phone down. Paranoia set in, so I ran back to the bathroom, picked up the sponge, and scrubbed furiously. I had to get hold of that letter, there was no way around it. I knew where Bel kept her writing materials, but I wasn't even sure if the letter still existed. Maybe she'd burned it, or given it to Mama, but knowing Bel, she'd probably held on to it. She'd hidden it somewhere. Bel was a pack rat of the first order. There was never anything in her wastebasket but Kleenex.

She had the largest room upstairs, an ensuite with its own bathroom. Mama took possession of the smaller room diagonally across from the master suite. It had a large window looking out over the backyard. Charlie and Zack shared the bedroom across from Bel at the front of the house, and they also shared Mama's bathroom. Jeffrey and I had the basement to ourselves. It was partly finished, with two small bedrooms, a bathroom, and a large, uninviting rec room with a red tile floor and no furniture. None of us fit into the house except for Bel. She had red checkered curtains on her window overlooking the street and the purple foothills to the west. She inherited Grandma's writing desk and bought herself a secondhand chaise lounge, which I envied even more than that desk. I could have read double the volume of novels, if I'd only had that chaise. Bel slept in both of her twin beds. I don't know why. It was just in her nature to alternate between them every week.

I had a tough time getting into her room, because I had school during the week, and she had quit teaching for a few years. Mama stayed home on the weekends, and it was too risky to sneak in when they were downstairs. My opportunity came about two weeks after the phone conversation, on a Saturday. The boys were outside, and Mama and Bel had gone downtown to look at drapes for the living room.

Bel's desk was the most obvious place to start, but I didn't hold out much hope of finding anything in so conspicuous a place. I rifled through the envelopes and letters stuck in the compartments under the slide top but didn't find anything significant except bills and grocery lists. Why Bel kept five years' worth of grocery lists, I'll never know, but there they were, all bundled up and held together with a rubber band. I also found some folders of crudely drawn thank-you notes from the kids she'd taught. No doubt a year-end assignment, judging from the quantity.

I had an idea where Bel would keep something personal. I felt like a sneak going through her chest of drawers, but I knew darn well that if she hadn't destroyed the letter, I'd find it there. And I did. I found a fat packet of letters, stuffed into an envelope, right between her sockettes and her D-cups.

Most of them were from Roland. I didn't read them. I figured I'd save those ones for another time. But stashed in the middle of the bundle were two letters from Papa. I was so nervous my hands got all clammy, and I had to swing them in the air before I replaced the packet, shut the drawer, and headed back to the bathroom with my treasure.

The first letter from Papa, dated December 2, 1961, was to inform Aunt Bel that he'd been in hospital for a month. Mama wouldn't tell her, he wrote, because she was too proud. It was scrawled all over the page and hard to read. He asked Bel to keep an eye on Mama, maybe give her a call or write to her because she was going through hell.

I had the feeling when I opened that second plump letter that there was no going back after I read it; that it contained something I didn't want to hear. So, I sat on the toilet seat and stared at it for a long time, trying to decide whether I'd be better off just putting it back and forgetting about it. In the end, I couldn't.

December 27, 1961

Dear Isabel:

I'm back home now, recovering. Thanks for calling Maddy, I think it meant a lot to her. She's started working part-time which is helping out because the doctor told me to spend at least another month at home.

It happened quickly, without any warning. This probably won't be the last I'll hear from my heart. I'm about to take you into my confidence and so I trust you won't breathe a word of this unless I die and it becomes necessary. But if I recover from this, which I intend to do, I'll tell Maddy myself. Now you be clear on that, Isabel.

You know we adopted Zack five years ago, in October, and I'm sure you also know that Maddy and I had some problems for a while before Zack arrived. I'm not going into details here, but things were pretty miserable at home. Maddy was overwhelmed with the kids and she had no time for her art. We had too many kids too fast, and though I wouldn't send any of them back, if I could do it over again, I'd stop listening to the Catholic Church.

Here's what you need to know. I got into a relationship with someone at the bank. It was my fault, I pursued her. The affair was discreet and short-lived, but she got pregnant. She wanted an abortion, and it cost me a lot of time and effort to persuade her otherwise. Her father had money and he could pay to send her to a good physician. But I couldn't have that on my conscience.

37

I told Madeline that a trainee at the bank had "discovered" that she was pregnant and in a real mess. I said that she was intent on having an abortion by any means, and I had been trying to talk her out of it. Maddy agreed that the girl shouldn't seek an abortion. It was too dangerous. As you probably know, her good friend Connie had died the year before trying to give herself an abortion and Maddy felt guilty that she could have done more. Anyway, we had a big discussion about all the options and eventually she came to the decision herself. We've already got three, why not four, she said. I could have given her a hundred reasons for "why not four" but I was looking out for my own interests.

I know you've had your suspicions, Bel, so now you can stop remarking on how much Zack looks like me. I don't want you to tell Maddy because I intend to, but if I die suddenly, I am entrusting this knowledge to you. If you do have to tell her, please let her down gently, and meanwhile, I beg you not to hold this secret over her head.

Some things in life humble us, and this is certainly one of them.

Yours truly,
Jon

I sat on the toilet for a long time and tried to imagine this side of Papa's personality, but there was a big black hole in my head. All I could think of was Mama. How alone she must have been after Papa's death. To Bel's credit, she had come through with some support when the chips were down, but I don't think Mama could push their new intimacy too far. I couldn't imagine Bel humbling herself in any way. I had the feeling that she reveled in being privy to this deceit. She always wanted to have power over Mama and her concerns, and Papa handed it to her on a silver platter. It made me angry that he didn't level with Mama before he died. She didn't deserve this ... did she? No, she married Papa in good faith, lived through his moods, struggled through thick and thin. Papa had buried this lie for years, and it only came out when he thought he might be dying. Feelings I'd never experienced before swirled inside me, and the room spun around until I thought I was going to pass out. I stuck my head between my legs and a screech went off in the black spaces of my brain.

As a kid, I used to have this daydream about a dragon. I don't know when it started, but I must have been pretty young. I guess somebody read me a book about a dragon, and it burst off the page and into my mind and stayed there, all through my childhood. The dragon had a wide grin and lived inside a cave with hundreds of rooms. As time went on, I saw that he really wasn't anything to be afraid of, and I started calling him Poof. We would hang out together. He wanted to hear stories, and I wanted to hear him wax philosophical. The only thing I didn't like was that he didn't invite himself into my imagination. Instead, he and his cave world would just burst into my mind, and I couldn't stop him from doing that.

Now it was happening again, only this time, the dragon and I were in the cave watching a mighty whirlwind churn outside. It stripped all the leaves off the trees and tore the bushes from their roots. Then the rain started. It beat harder and harder until the pellets of water turned to hail. I couldn't get out of the cave, and I panicked. I looked back at Poof hoping that he could help. But something was happening to his face. His eyes glowed like red coals, his nostrils quivered, his teeth grew fangs, and suddenly he lunged at me, snarling and snorting fumes. I ran out into the storm, ran and ran through the briars and the bushes and the black pines until my legs were too numb to carry me farther.

I woke up in a sweat on the bathroom floor. I raced to return the letter, and then I'm not sure what happened, but I managed to get downstairs to my bedroom. I had a high fever that kept me from school until Wednesday of the following week. The dream was so real I convinced myself that I caught the cold out there in the storm.

There were no more dragon dreams after that. But every time I went to bed, I'd try to stay awake as long as I could so that my mind wouldn't let the dragon in. Only once did I catch a glimpse of him coming around a corner in a big old mansion, and I turned up the TV so loud that everybody started yelling at me. I shut the TV off, and that shut off the dream. In my late teens, the dragon reinvaded my mind for a couple of years. He entreated me as if he had something he wanted to tell me, but I ran away in terror. One day, I put a stop to the chase by turning around and slashing his throat with my fantasy dagger. Ear to ear, just like his grin. I resolved that I would never run from anything after that.

I returned the letters to their rightful place and didn't breathe a word about them to anyone. Over the weeks that followed, I think Mama sensed that I knew something, because I'd slide into trances and stare at her for long periods of time. She'd snap me out of them by returning my look with a startled, probing expression. Once I didn't turn away, I just looked her hard in the eyes and smiled sadly. I'm sure she knew that I knew about Zack.

A few days after I'd read Papa's letter, Jeffrey and Charlie came down to my room after school. They knocked, which was unusual, and barged in, which wasn't. Jeffrey demanded to know what was up. "There's something weird going on," he said. I sat up on my bed and fluffed the pillow. It was rather nice to be sought out as the expert in these matters, and the two of them looked so perplexed that I waited a moment to give the situation the gravity it deserved.

"C'mon, Alice, you can tell us. What's happening?"

Jeffrey launched himself onto the other twin bed as if he thought it was a trampoline. Charlie tried to do the same, except he didn't make it and he slipped off, bringing the covers and Jeffrey down with him. They threw the covers back on the bed and started the whole process over again. Jeffrey looked put off, and he gave Charlie a shove. I just rolled my eyes, thinking how dumb and goofy boys were.

I had to tell them something, or I'd never get them out of my room. Besides, I decided, they deserved to be given some idea. They were old enough.

"Well," I began. "Something's come out. Something that we weren't ever supposed to know."

Their eyes widened. Charlie scrambled around on the bed to get settled, crossed his legs, and rested his chin on his fists.

"You have to promise not to say anything to anybody about this. Especially Zack. Swear?"

They swore.

"Well, it seems that Zack … was adopted."

A loaded silence. Jeffrey looked up and frowned. "How come we didn't know?"

I thought for a moment about how I was going to string this lie. "Cause Mama didn't want it to change the way we treated him, and she didn't want him to feel different from the rest of us."

Jeffrey nodded, thinking hard. Charlie just kept staring at me with his eyes popping out. Then, in his tinker's voice, he blurted, "Is he the only one?"

"Yes, I'm positive about that," I said, but his question took me aback and made us all think twice. Even Jeffrey looked at him incredulously and then back at me. "Why did they adopt Zack when they already had the three of us?"

"Yeah," Charlie nodded furiously. "How come?"

I sighed as if to indicate that the answer was self-explanatory, and that I was getting impatient with their stupidity.

"Cause Mama didn't think she'd be able to have another baby, that's why. And she wanted at least four."

It was a safe response. My brothers thought I was privy to all the mysteries of womanhood when, in fact, I really didn't have the foggiest idea how the mechanics worked, much less how they'd break down.

Jeffrey nodded intelligently, and so did Charlie. I advised them to be careful about not treating Zack any differently, and to let Mama tell him the truth when she was good and ready. They bought that. They didn't ask any more questions. Yep, they just took hold of what I gave them, the same way I grabbed that rope swing, without ever thinking to ask about the seat or the knots. They'd have to find out for themselves, I thought, feeling much better as they trooped out of my room. Then I went upstairs to help Bel fix supper.

CHAPTER 3

THE LONG FALL

There was nothing geeky or awkward about my older brother Jeffrey. He went from being a boy to a man without so much as a pimple or a patch of fuzz. When he got to high school, he dropped the Montgomery surname and took my mother's name instead. He became Jeff Duval or J.D. for short. He never went anywhere without a bevy of cheerleaders bouncing around him, going gaga and giving him A's.

I don't know what the fascination was with cheerleaders. I threw away my Barbie dolls about the same time that I became conscious that there was a particularly dizzy variant of humankind called the "cheerleader". There was nothing subtle about them. I preferred the independent, neurotic types who'd wander around on the sidelines, sit under a tree and open a book. You never knew what was going on in their world. They belonged to an entirely higher order than all those legs and pom-poms that give good women a bad name. But then, I wasn't a boy—

something that was becoming certain fast. Too fast. I wasn't ready to spring into the world in my first pair of high heels, carrying my adulthood like a flag.

Jeffrey was an athlete from the cradle. I don't think he had to crawl to learn how to walk. He just stood up and strode out of the room. He had the knack of knowing how to make his body speak for him, how to carry himself with just enough subtlety to move the mountain in any direction he wished.

Naturally he was proud of his solid body. By Grade Ten he was broad shouldered and just tall enough to attract the medium-sized girls in dainty sandals and pumps, and avoid being coveted by the lanky ones like me who looked straight down from the neck, forever nailed to the earth in clumpy Oxfords.

Mostly, though, it was the fire in his eyes that excited the girls. He had Papa's eyes, deep-set with long, dark lashes. But whereas Papa's eyes were magnetic, Jeffrey's flashed with a peculiar, almost dangerous intensity. Females treated him with a submissive mixture of fear and giddiness, which revolted me long before I'd figured out the reason why. Jeffrey exuded restlessness—even his square jaw looked like it had been chiseled in a hurry, but females considered his unfinished good looks devastating. When his moustache appeared in Grade Eleven, he was "fatal", as they said. Depending on the company and his mood, of course, because Jeffrey was as moody as mountain weather. You were never quite at ease around him, you'd always be eyeing the sky for clouds. It was the price any girl would have to pay to be up high where the air was thin and intoxicating.

Zack adored Jeffrey. Papa's death severed an intimate physical bond between Zack and his Papa. Papa held baby Zack more than all the rest of us put together. I used to think that Papa clung to Zack because he didn't get enough physical affection from Mama. She never had enough of herself to spread around. She could no more reach us with her love than a pat of butter could cover a loaf of bread.

After Papa died, Zack switched his affection to Jeffrey. He followed him everywhere, and at first Jeffrey didn't mind having a protégé. He taught his youngest brother a lot, including how to handle a ball.

Zack had some of Jeffrey's agility, and because he was leaner, he had a kind of artful grace that I think even Jeffrey envied a little. It was clear to all of us, though, that Zack's admiration for Jeffrey amounted to idolatry. When he got into the middle of his teens, Jeffrey started to take advantage of Zack's admiration. One day I heard the two of them talking in Jeffrey's room. Jeffrey was bargaining.

"Okay, so next week, if you do the vacuuming for me, I'll let you into the game on Friday."

"I want short stop," Zack said.

"No can do. Centre field is my best offer."

"I'm the best short stop you've got."

"You don't like the offer, then don't play the game."

"You're a shit, Jeffrey."

"Does that mean you'll play?"

Laughter. From Jeffrey.

A little later on, Zack came down for dinner while I was making the salad. I said, "You know Jeffrey's just using you, right?"

He went around to the fridge. "To do what?"

"His chores."

He pulled out a bottle of ranch dressing and set it on the counter beside the cutting board where I was working. "Put my dressing on the side, Alice."

My anger flared. "I'm not your servant, Zack."

I had wanted to say, "Jeffrey's an idiot if he doesn't see how good you are," but it wasn't possible now. He watched me cut the tomatoes, a sheen of tears in his eyes. Before I could figure out how to bridge the miles between us, Bel came into the kitchen.

When Jeffrey got on the high school football team in Grade Ten, no one was as proud as Zack. He went to every game. He didn't mind being on the sidelines and having to compete with Jeffrey's other admirers. Still, the one person he couldn't compete with was Brenda, who came into the picture at the end of the school year in 1966.

Brenda Robertson was the best-looking cheerleader at Mount Regent High. Everybody knew her by name. I figured she'd have as many titles to prom queen as she'd later have husbands. She had white blonde hair that bounced on her shoulders and gleamed in the sunlight. She told everyone that her mother had been an aristocrat in Romania, and she affected a slight accent to go along with the rest of her charms. She was all perfume and boobs, bangles and nails.

For a whole year in Grade Ten, she suffocated Jeff in English class with a cumulus cloud of Yves St. Laurent. He ignored her for months, but she worked on him steadily—an ankle here, a little cleavage there, and the constant *ting-ting* of earrings and bracelets.

I think he succumbed in the fall of Grade Eleven. The Regent team had just won its third game in a row and everything was coming up roses. Brenda, her blonde hair flying in the wind, came bounding up to Jeffrey while Zack and I were loitering around, thinking of interesting things to say.

It was an easy moment to steal. Jeffrey and I stood there and gawked at her. No getting around it, she was a knockout. She had almost exotic blue eyes and clear porcelain skin, not a blemish to comfort me. I'm positive that the look Jeffrey took then was the deciding one. You could almost feel his pupils dilate. Zack had started to say something, but we all forgot to listen to him. He snapped his mouth shut, gave Jeffrey a disgusted pout, and stalked off. Brenda, her deep V promising the eighth and ninth wonders of the world, hugged Jeffrey's arm and gave me a not-too-discreet signal to get lost. I grinned stiffly and stood my ground.

"Oh Jay Deeee," she gushed. "This team would be nothing without you. I mean, sure Eddie's fast, and he can hold onto the ball, but he doesn't understand the game like you do. He missed a lot of opportunities out there, don't you think?" She eyed me condescendingly and swung her head back up to Jeffrey. With a maturity that tripled her years, she said, "You keep playing like that, J.D. and you'll be quarterback in no time."

I found the whole scene nauseating, and I was just about to take off when I caught sight of something so astonishing, I nearly tripped over my clodhoppers. True to character, I didn't think, I just poked my finger at Brenda's chest and gasped. "Oh, no, Brenda. Look! Your stuffing's coming out!" Sure enough, bursting out of the deep V, was a real elephant-sized wad of Kleenex. She spun away from Jeffrey like a fireball and hollered, "Get rid of your sister, mister!" as she fled.

There was a sudden silence among the crowd left on the field. Jeffrey grabbed me by the shoulders and shook me hard. "What the hell's the matter with you, Alice!" My hand was still on my mouth, but the awful thing was out, and there was no putting it back. Then Jeffrey cracked up, and we laughed so hard I leaked. Brenda was long gone, thank God. But she'd be back. I knew it, and he knew it.

By the end of Jeffrey's year in Grade Eleven, it looked as if Brenda's prophesy would come true. There were bigger guys than Jeffrey on the team, but they moved around on the field like Neanderthals, whereas Jeffrey could duck and run quick as a flare, and he could throw the football nearly half the length of the field. He studied the game too, like a science. It was a peak year for him and, I might add, for Brenda, whom he started to date before the first snow. I wasn't too enamored with the drippy side of Jeffrey, if truth be told. It put him out of focus somehow and took the certainty out of his stride.

But poor Zack! Jeffrey shook him off like a sticky brown leaf and spent most of his spare time off skiing with Brenda, whose parents had a chalet in Canmore. Zack sat around in the house and moped until January, when he revived and got himself a paper route. Zack never did anything except in extremes. He took on two routes. From four o'clock until long after dark he'd be out stumbling along in the snow, covering three and a half square miles to get his flyers delivered. Mama kept his supper waiting until he got back, but she didn't keep him from doing what he set out to do. She said Zack could handle it, and if he couldn't, well then, he'd stop. There were a few blizzards that winter, though, and that's when Mama got Jeffrey to drive him along in the car. Jeffrey resented the consignment, and on a bitterly cold night at the end of January, Jeffrey and Zack had a fight. Jeffrey opened the passenger door and ordered Zack to stuff the rest of his papers down the sewer grate. Zack stepped out into the blizzard, fiercely protesting. Jeffrey threw the sack of newspapers at him so hard that he fell into a snowbank, and then Jeffrey drove away.

In the end, Zack's diligence paid off. By the end of March, he had made close to a hundred dollars in wages and tips. One Saturday afternoon in early April, he conspired with Mama, and she took him out somewhere in the car. He came back with a box, looking positively triumphant, and disappeared upstairs.

I went into the kitchen to set the table. When Mama came in and swept her apron off the hook, I thought she might start dancing around the room with all the excitement packed into her. "What's going on?" I asked. "Did I just see Zack smiling?" He was such a serious kid, very private, and in control of every little thing he possessed.

"Can't say." She hung the white apron over her neck and tied it behind her back. "Sometimes he reminds me of your father. Can you hand me those gloves?" I passed her the yellow gloves she used for dishwashing, and she reached for the oatmeal pot that had been sitting in the sink since breakfast. "They're men of grand gestures," she said, dumping out the swill. "Infrequent, but grand."

I thought maybe Zack had a date or something. He didn't come back downstairs until Mama began serving the spaghetti. He pulled out his chair and sat down without saying anything to anybody. He looked a bit disheveled, which might be normal for most twelve-year-olds, but not Zack. He liked his straight dark hair cut close, longer in the front but never past his ears. Tonight, though, strands of hair kept falling into his eyes. He'd swipe them off his forehead with the back of his hand, but they would fall again and stick. He was clearly sweating.

Mama took her time serving the meal, first the spaghetti, and then the salad. Normally we would just pass the bowls around, but tonight had become formal. "Is somebody coming for dinner?" Charlie asked.

"Nope," said Mama.

When we had finished our tapioca pudding, Mama said, "Now before you go anywhere, Zack has a little presentation to make." Zack popped out of his chair and ran upstairs. *Thump, thump, thump* over the top of us, and *thump, thump, thump* all the way down. He reappeared holding a big box wrapped in tissue paper and tied with a fat green satin ribbon. Jeffrey was sitting across from him with his elbows on the table. He'd been surly all the way through dinner, probably because of some fight with Brenda. Zack slid the box across to Jeffrey, and then he leaned back in his chair and crossed his arms. His cheeks were flaming. Jeffrey sat up, looking baffled.

"What's this, Zack?"

He pulled on the ribbon, and it untied itself and fell to the sides of the box. He tore off the tissue paper and lifted the cover. Inside the box sat a baseball glove made of genuine leather.

Zack's eyes were gleaming like stars. Jeffrey stared at the glove for several long seconds, without either removing it from the package or saying anything. Finally, he looked up at Zack.

"Did you spend *all* your paper money on this?"

Zack straightened his back, proud as could be, and nodded. "Yup. Well, most of it, anyway."

"Then you're a damn fool." Jeffrey shoved the box into the middle of the table. Zack frowned, and it looked as though he might start to cry.

"I don't play baseball anymore, Zack." Jeffrey glared at him. "I play football. And besides, you've got your own life to live. Stop living mine. I don't want your stupid glove."

He yanked himself out of the chair and stalked out, leaving the glove behind. Zack got up, went around the table, and picked up his trophy. His fingers were trembling. They looked delicate in that moment, almost like a woman's, and tears were slipping down his cheeks. He didn't say anything. He just took the box away upstairs.

Jeffrey was twelve when Papa died and the family moved to Calgary. He took it all very hard, but no one knew exactly how hard because he made himself scarce. One night in the fall, a few months after we moved, he threw a tantrum downstairs in his bedroom. Right out of the blue. He demolished all the model submarines he had spent years building as a kid. He stomped on them and hurled the pieces at the wall, roaring at the top of his lungs. Then he went out, no one knew where. Mama went down to his bedroom and sat there until three in the morning when he came in. Jeffrey's room was in the basement, right next door to mine, so I heard the whole thing.

At that time, Mama wasn't really fit to handle anything. She looked so thin and pale that I worried she might follow Papa to the grave and leave us at the mercy of Bel. When Jeffrey came into his room, she demanded to know where he'd been. She sounded more exhausted than angry. I heard a long silence and thought she might have passed out. Then I heard her sobbing. When Jeffrey tried to comfort her, she told him that she needed him, that he was the man in the house now. She couldn't make it on her own, not without his support. It was very painful listening to her cry like that. She was a proud woman, and she rarely let her feelings show. When she finished, there was a long, icy pause. The bed creaked.

"What was that you said?" Mama asked. Her voice was quiet.

"I said I hate him. I *hate* him."

"Oh, come on, Jeffrey. You don't mean that."

"I'll never forgive him. Ever."

"For what? For dying?"

"For being weak. He's a coward, if you wanna know what I think. He took the easy way out. He always did."

"What do you mean, Jeffrey?"

At first there was no answer. Then he said, "He had obligations! Why didn't he fight for us? He just turned into a zombie like he did before!"

"You're going to call him that when he's hardly gone cold in his grave?"

Mama got up and started for the door. "You've got some pretty high expectations, young man. I hope life doesn't disappoint you. But I won't have you speaking that way about your father. He was a good man, and I adored him."

Mama left the room and I heard Jeffrey mutter, "Yeah, the moon and the stars and all that crap...."

I could feel Mama lingering in the hallway. She opened my door softly and poked her head in to see if I was sleeping. I squeezed my eyes shut. She stood there for what seemed like forever.

Zack continued delivering papers all through that hot, windless summer. He joined a little league baseball team, and never once spoke to Jeffrey, if he could avoid it. For his part, Jeffrey sniffed around Brenda until he got himself trapped. I think he made some attempt to escape, but by late summer he looked downright caged. One day in August, Mama got a phone call from his coach who told her that Jeffrey hadn't been to practice for two weeks. He asked Mama if there were family problems or something he ought to know about. She said there were none that she knew of. He told her that Jeffrey had blown his chances to be quarterback, and "he better have a damn fine excuse or I don't want him back. You tell him that, you hear?" That was the beginning of a long fall.

It only aggravated the situation that Zack refused to acknowledge Jeffrey's existence. Zack never went to a game. No one did. And since Jeffrey wasn't talking, it wasn't clear where he stood with the team. I discovered from a friend of Brenda's that he was taken back after a furor with the coach, and then got his walking papers in mid-September. "Nice job breaking the quarterback," I wanted to say to Brenda, but I kept my mouth shut.

I avoided her as much as I could and only tolerated her presence if we got thrown together in the same room. I didn't trust her. She hung around with the prettiest (and meanest) girls in the school, and I guess she didn't trust me either, because I had a bad habit of saying what was on my mind, usually at the wrong time. So it had to have been a crisis that drove her to track me down in the cafeteria one rainy day in October. I was standing at the lunch counter, holding my tray. I'd just received a mound of meatloaf and mashed potatoes when Brenda kicked the side of my shoe. "Alice. I need to talk to you." She was wearing an oversized navy cardigan and she had nothing on her tray but a bottle of juice and a milk carton.

"Sure, okay," I said. I followed her to a spot at the end of a long table and we pulled out our chairs.

She doffed her sweater, revealing an ivory V-neck blouse that showed her cleavage under a gold chain with a ruby heart. She pursed her lips in a kissy way that made her look a bit demented and actually scared me a little. Then she shook her glistening mane.

"Okay, now you need to tell me what's happened to your brother."

Her tone was so offensive that I reacted. "What do you think we do? Beat him every night and hang him upside down from a meat hook?" I took hold of my tray and slid back my chair to go. She grabbed my arm, toppling her juice bottle.

"Sorry, Alice. I didn't mean to come on so strong." She set her juice bottle upright. I noticed a tremor in her hand, and I thought maybe she was going to tell me she was pregnant.

"I'm just trying to understand what happened. J.D. had such a great thing going. He was, like, the star of the team, right? And then he messed the whole thing up, and he won't even tell me why!" She stabbed her straw into the milk carton and sucked till the carton was dry. The milk seemed to comfort her, and she sat back, winding her long nyloned legs around one another. She really was quite beautiful. Like a cat.

"We were so close, you can't imagine. We were planning a life together. Then suddenly he goes cold and throws the whole thing away. It's like he died, you know." She levelled me with her doll eyes. "Well?"

"Well, what?"

"What's going on, Alice? Is there, like, some kind of problem at home?" Her voice had become shrill and I could tell by their smirks that the boys at the table next to us were listening.

"I don't have a clue what you're talking about."

She banged her tray on the table which got the attention of the whole cafeteria.

"Stop acting so stupid, Alice. Why is your brother making me look like such an idiot?"

"I think you're doing that all on your own, Brenda."

"Don't you get it? We were planning our wedding!"

"What?"

"It was all arranged! We rented the ballroom at the Banff Springs and everything. I even bought my dress!"

She started rocking back and forth like she had to pee. "I know what happened. I've been suspecting it all along."

"Suspecting what?"

She thrust her chin at me. "Do you know who he talks about all the time? Do you know who I have to compete with? Do you have any idea?"

"Uh—"

"Your mother! I mean, what is it with your mother? Is he in love with her or something? That's pretty twisted, don't you think?"

I shoved my tray of cold meatloaf into hers and stood up. "You start spreading rumors like that, Brenda Robertson, and I'll break your face."

"My family has money, you know. They could have started us out right, if your brother hadn't turned into such a fairy."

I started to walk away.

"Don't think for one second that my family is going to let him off the hook!" she shouted. "We're going to make him pay!"

"You go ahead and do that," I said, walking down the aisle between rows of tables. Everybody had gone silent. I fixed my eyes on the cafeteria doors.

"Your brother's got a serious complex, Alice! Everybody knows it. Jeff Duval's a fag!"

I whirled around. "Yeah, and you've got Kleenex for boobs!" The cafeteria erupted in whoops of laughter as I made my exit, punching through the swinging doors.

I had to talk to Jeffrey. Things were falling apart around him, and he was buried under all that debris. I wanted to do something to help him, even though I knew darn well that any overture could be dangerous. The following week, on a Friday night, I managed to get ahold of a jug of Donini wine, and asked Jeffrey to meet me in the tree fort that my brothers had built into the old maple near the ravine.

He showed up around nine, and we went through a couple of mugs in silence before I got the nerve to ask him about Brenda.

"That's been a mess for a long time," he said. He lit a cigarette. He was cool as the moonlight that poured in through the door space, and I had a flooding, pleasant sensation of being a mouse in a tree hole, secure for a moment in a big, crazy world. There was nothing in the box fort except for an old soup can that served as an ashtray, a candle stub, and a carton of nails. The light was picking up reddish threads in Jeffrey's crop of curly brown hair.

"She wanted everything her way. She didn't give me any space." He drew hard on his cigarette and blew the smoke out the doorway.

"No one gives me any space." He glared at me accusingly. "I'm tired of having people make some kinda god outta me. I'm fed up with having to meet everybody's expectations. Brenda had her own fairy tale going. I couldn't stop it once it started." I could see him grinding his teeth, the jaw bones popping in and out.

He grinned. "I heard about the scene she made in the cafeteria."

"Positively Shakespearian," I said.

"Yeah, well nothing's worth that nightmare." He picked up the can and crushed out his cigarette. "I'll tell you something, Alice. I can't handle this place anymore. I can't breathe."

I was finding it hard to breathe, myself.

"I get it from all sides. You know that Zack hasn't said one word to me since he tried to give me that stupid glove?" He knocked back the rest of his wine. "I'm not going to carry the ball for anyone anymore. I've got my own life to live."

"I get it, Jeff. But you really hurt Zack by throwing that glove back in his face."

"It's not like I don't know that, Alice. Jesus. Of all people, I didn't want to hurt Zack. I know he's not blood, but he reminds me of Papa. Something about him. He walks the same way. He's got the same authority over people. He's always had it and I've admired it.

"Then, all of a sudden, he wants me to set the pace for him. Starts imitating me, living his whole life for me. Maybe I would have preferred it the other way around." His voice turned icy. "That glove shoulda taught him a lesson."

I refilled his mug. Just then, Zack called up from the base of the tree.

Now I don't want to admit to having schemes of my own—and I was taking a big risk with this one—but I had mentioned that bottle of wine to Zack and I'd invited him to help me polish it off. When he called up, Jeffrey poked his head out beside mine. Zack froze, stepped away, and crossed his arms in defiance.

"Hey, little brother!" Jeffrey slurred. "Why don't you come on up?"

Zack glared at me. "No thanks." The wind had picked up and he was clutching his light jacket.

Jeffrey got to his feet with some difficulty and pushed me away from the doorway.

"Come on up and imbibe."

"I only drink with friends." Zack turned to leave.

"What'd you say?" Jeffrey scrambled down a couple of tree slats and then jumped the rest of the way, supported by a low branch. Reeling a little, he put his arm around Zack's shoulders. "Let's just forget it, okay little bro?"

Zack shook him off. "I'm not in the mood," he muttered. He started to head off, and Jeffrey blew his cool.

"You wanna punch me out? Huh? Is that what you want? Then do it, you bastard. Get it outta your system! I'm sick of your sulking and crap. Show me what you've got!"

Zack just kept on walking. Jeffrey bellowed, "You want me to be your old man, do you? Well we gotta go it alone, fella. Cause we don't have an old man. And maybe *you* never had one!"

Zack wheeled around. "You think that's gonna hurt me? Well, let me tell you something, Jeffrey. I've known that piece of news for a long time. And a whole lot more. That's the difference between you and me, *bro*. I can face the truth about myself. You can't." They stood there in a stalemate, facing one another about twenty feet apart, Jeffrey looking for all the world like a drugged bear, and Zack, a slim shadow rooted to the ground like a tough sapling.

Jeffrey belched out a laugh and sprang into action. He charged Zack and tackled him. Brought him down hard, slamming Zack's right shoulder into the ground.

For a second neither of them moved. Then Zack got to his feet, holding his shoulder.

Jeffrey stayed on the ground, sobbing. "Jesus Christ, I'm sorry, Zack. Goddammit I'm sorry." I backed into the shadows of the tree fort. After a few minutes, he went quiet. I peered outside.

Zack stood over Jeffrey, waiting for him to get it out of his system. Jeffrey sat up and wiped his nose on his sleeve. Then Zack said, "I don't need you anymore, Jeff *Duval*." He shook out his injured shoulder and walked away.

Jeffrey fell back on the ground and stared up at the night sky … free as the dead.

CHAPTER 4

OUTSIDE THE BIG OAK DOORS

A unt Bel always prided herself on being able to spot
what she called "character" in people. In her view,
that elusive but decidedly obvious quality separated
the good from the bad, the chosen from the unchosen.
People who didn't have character weren't worth a damn,
in Bel's books. As far as the Montgomery family was
concerned, Bel kept her observations to herself, and
we didn't much care where she had us pegged. When
it came to outsiders, though, evaluation was inevitable,
and no matter how fast you tried to whisk your friend
past her in the hall, Bel never failed to halt you, milk a
little history from the poor victim, and make her indel-
ible pronouncement.

But this is Mama's story, and already Bel is intruding,
right off the top. Well, I suppose Mama wouldn't be
herself without Bel flying in and out of her life on a

broomstick, breaking Mama's spirit and giving her a chronic case of nervous hysteria. Still, family is family. When the chips were down, blood flowed to blood. And maybe, though I never caught a whiff of any compatibility between the two women, Isabel couldn't keep herself away from the light at the center of all our lives. I'll go to my grave believing that no one, not even Bel, who could sometimes get downright predatory, could do anything but protect that flame.

It makes my stomach flutter to think about Mama. When I was a little girl, I saw her as a storybook character—a landlocked mermaid in a long white apron with deep pockets that fluttered when she passed. On a whim, she could snap her fingers and turn an ordinary moment into magic—doff her work clothes and come downstairs in a party dress, ready to go out dancing.

Papa wasn't much of a dancer, but Mama could get him moving in the living room when she felt like putting on some jazz. "Let's have some jazz, Jon," she'd sing, and it didn't matter how tired or grouchy he was. By the time she'd undone her apron strings, he'd be walking into her arms.

She wouldn't always be that way. I had to get older to realize that Mama was a puzzle in a box with no picture on the cover, and many tiny pieces inside. You could start anywhere putting Mama's story together, and it's a little dizzying at the outset. At the heart of the picture was a studio, way up on the third floor of our house in

Toronto, where we lived until I was ten. Mama's studio is a piece of the puzzle that I carry with me everywhere, like a talisman.

To get to Mama's studio, you had to climb the narrow staircase up to the third floor. At the top you'd come to a landing with a hardwood floor and an oak railing that let you peek downstairs. The banister was carved with acorns and oak leaves. Even though I was intruding on Mama's hiding place, I made that magic corner mine. You could tune into what was going on down below without being caught in the middle of the drama. You were never seen, and a little stained glass window, with a stylized rose nestled in yellow and green foliage, gave you enough light to read under. I would huddle there for hours like the town urchin while Mama busied herself in her private studio behind two big oak doors.

Every now and then, Mama would let me in, usually during cleanup. She would toss me a wet sponge, and I'd wipe the counters or scrub muck off the floor. Her studio was gabled and had leaded-pane windows looking south. Mama had made the glass windows herself in a pattern of ferns. Below them, a long cedar slab held her flowers and potted plants, all flourishing in unfired clay pots.

If she wasn't ready to clean up, Mama would let me play with her drawing and painting materials. They were all shelved on the north side of the room, next to her drawing table. She'd give me a piece of paper from the stacks on the shelves and let me paint on the floor. She never minded if things got messy because we always had that big blue sponge to do the mopping up. The only area that was out of bounds to all children was her elegant old bookcase with glass doors. It held her proudest accomplishment: three bronzed dancing figures she had made as a college student. If you wanted to see them, you would have to ask permission, and she would unlock the cabinet. Holding one in your hands, even a child could see that Mama had a special feel for how bodies move and join. Two male dancers stretched toward one another, creating a dome over a female figure in the middle who rose like a flame between them, and reached beyond the space they had made for her. All three dancers were faceless, although their sex was obvious, and the pieces could stand together or apart. It was a breathtaking work of art, the best thing Mama ever did. Everything else seemed to be struggling back to it.

Mama did her sculpting at the work counter and sink opposite the bookcase. I would shriek with delight when she sliced through the clay. I can still feel the sensual pleasure of that wire cutting through the smooth, solid muck.

Aside from making pots and bowls, Mama used that lovely raw clay to produce weird little creatures that looked like they had just crawled out of a swamp. They had reptilian faces, and squat humanoid bodies, and they were strewn all over the place in her studio. Papa affectionately called them Mama's "lizzies". With their little hungry eyes and wide mouths, they served effectively to ward off small children.

Once, when Charlie was three, Mama had him on her lap when she was sitting at her desk. He reached for a milk jug of paintbrushes, and when he moved it, he saw the lizzie crouching behind it. He screamed like his hand had been bitten by a snake. Mama carried him, shrieking, downstairs. "That's a bad think you did, Mama! A bad think!"

I wasn't scared of Mama's lizzies, but they enhanced my feeling that her studio was a sacred place where children were not allowed except by invitation, and where Mama could be entirely in possession of herself.

Every time Bel swooped in for a visit, thunderclouds gathered, but her stays never lasted long enough to be threatening. Papa protected Mama like one of her own lizzies and prevented her from being hurt by folks like Bel whose tongues and opinions ruled with all the subtlety of a rock hammer. As Papa would say, Mama needed the right touch. When she was happy, she flourished like one of her potted plants, and she had a way of making you feel an almost painful kind of ease.

Then Papa died. It was as catastrophic for the Montgomery family as the planet shifting on its axis. All of a sudden, the house went quiet. No meals. No nothing. Mama locked herself in her studio. The next day, Bel flew to Toronto. It was Bel who told us that Papa had collapsed on the subway. "Your Mama got a call from the police," she said. She was standing at the kitchen sink, rinsing plates under the tap water. "By that time, they had taken him to the morgue, and she had to go down and identify his body."

Bel wiped her hands on her apron and wagged her finger at us. "Now you kids are going to have to grow up fast, right here and now," she said. Poor little Zack, he was only five. I can still see him standing in the kitchen dangling Dolly by one foot. How was he supposed to grow up? "Everything's going to change, and the best way to support your Mama right now is to move along with the changes." She shivered her body like a serpent had taken possession of her. "Move like water."

Charlie bawled, "No, no!" and ran to his room. No way would he grow up.

But Bel was right, of course, and by the end of that tearful, rainy summer, we landed in the west, in a house in south Calgary that had all the character of a cereal box. With four of us to account for, Mama had her hands full the first few months after we arrived. I don't honestly know how she got through those days, how she enrolled us all in school, and where she got the strength to get herself two clerical jobs. I just figured she would die. She was too rare a plant. But she didn't. She packed up her life in Toronto, moved to a city she had never set foot in, and settled in with a relative she'd never been able to tolerate.

There were some pretty visible changes in her. She appeared to be ageing by the hour. She took to wearing thick face makeup to cover the dark rings under her eyes and hide the rash that had broken out around her nose and mouth. She rubbed on a harsh red lipstick that collided with her auburn hair. She lost weight, and the green flicker of light vanished from her eyes.

Everyone was naturally drawn to Mama's defense during that time. Even Bel was surprisingly compassionate. Although she had never been a slim woman, Bel seemed to grow even rounder, softer, more maternal. She quit teaching elementary school for a couple of years to help around the house. My older brother Jeffrey was suspicious of the transformation and resented Bel's attention to Mama. He was always watching for the hawk to reappear so he could fight her back. But Bel sweetened right up.

Still, Jeffrey guarded the gate. You had to pass him to cross over to Mama, and you weren't going anywhere with a complaint in your pocket or an accusation up your sleeve. When she got home from work, she would go up to the second floor to her room, and shut the door. Jeffrey would hang out in the living room. Every now and then he would bring her tea, or sometimes supper on a tray, if she wanted it. If Charlie saw Jeffrey going upstairs, he would say, "Are you going up to see Mama? Can I come? I'd like to see how she's feeling." When Mama was downstairs, Charlie would pop up around

71

every corner. "How are you feeling, Mama? Are you feeling better now? Do you need anything?" We were all driven around the bend by the repetition and the pitiful whine in his voice that made you think Charlie was in fact more hurt than Mama by Papa's death.

When we were firmly installed in school and something of a routine settled in, Mama's behavior didn't alter much. She seemed to have regained a certain control, at the expense of her spontaneity. You would think she was made of porcelain the way she propped herself up at the kitchen table in the morning. She would lean stiffly on one arm and ask what mothers are supposed to remember to ask, without the faintest glimmer of interest. "Did you do your homework, Alice? Did you brush your teeth, Charlie? Jeffrey, can you stop by the corner store and pick up some tuna fish? Aunt Bel forgot to put it on the list." "Yes, Mama. Sure, Mama. No problem, Mama." We were very polite at the breakfast table the first year after Papa died. We did what we were told and hoped that Mama would return to us. That became our first real act of faith, and we kept a vigil for signs of life under all that makeup and that porcelain doll face.

Mama had no studio in Calgary. There wasn't enough room to store her materials downstairs, so she let them go to a church sale. She held on to the dancers, but the lizzies went into the garbage bin. Mama kept a few watercolors of flowers and plants, but they weren't her best work. She stored them in the furnace room. "I miss your red calla lily," I said to her one night in November, a few months after we had moved. We had gathered in the living room. Mama and I were on the couch, and Bel was sitting in her old wingback chair, knitting under the light of a floor lamp.

"It would be perfect over there," Bel said, poking a needle in the direction of the bare wall opposite her.

"I couldn't look at it. It would make me sick," Mama said. She tucked her feet up under her dressing gown and propped her cheek on one hand. She had her hair up in rollers.

"Nonsense," Bel snapped. "It would brighten up the room. At the very least, we can put up some wallpaper."

The boys were sprawled on the floor watching Ed Sullivan, and Mama was getting annoyed by their outbursts of laughter.

"The wall doesn't need anything," I said. "It's fine as it is."

Mama threw me a grateful look. Bel continued to stab her needles into the purple wool. "I think it's tragic, absolutely tragic that you've stopped doing your art, Madeline. And don't tell me there isn't any room for a studio in the house. You have the entire rec room to work in. It's just standing there empty."

Empty, for good reason! It was a bleak windowless room in the basement—the least inspired room in a completely uninspired house. Bel went on. "I don't know why you gave it all away. Your paintings, especially. They were so original. How are you going to get your originality back?"

Mama winced, and Jeffrey shot up from the floor in his striped black and white pajamas that made him look like a convict.

"We don't need any paintings in our living room, Aunt Bel," he said, looking her dead in the eye. She chuckled dismissively, as if Jeffrey were a mere moth fluttering around the shade of her lamp.

Mama was visibly surprised at the gallant stance taken by her twelve-year-old. "Thanks, Jeffrey," she said. "Anyway, I'm too busy right now to think about my art."

"Well, that's it for me, I'm off to bed." Bel launched herself out her chair and shuffled off in her white fuzzy slippers that Charlie called "carpet slippers" because they looked like they were made out of a shag rug.

"Too-da-loo," Mama said. She smiled wearily. Charlie turned the TV off. "You'll have your studio again one day," I said, resting my head on her shoulder. She patted my thigh. Jeffrey came and squeezed in beside me, and then Charlie and Zack piled on. Mama didn't exactly cuddle us but letting us all sit packed together with her on the sofa was sufficient to kindle the promise that she would one day come back to us.

The long weeks of winter passed. A dreary Christmas, followed by a series of blizzards. Then, on February 13, before I'd even gotten up, Charlie came bounding into my room. "Alice, I got a great idea," he said, clambering onto my bed. He was wearing his red candy cane pajamas with the trap door and the feet, which he got at Christmas.

"Charlie, it's too early in the morning. And your breath stinks."

He crawled closer. "Let's get Mama a Valentine, Alice. They got them at Tucker Drugs. I saw them." He put his hand out and started counting imaginary money. "If you give me 25 cents, and you get Jeffrey to give me 25 cents, then maybe you can ask Aunt Bel to give us 50 cents, for her part and Zack's, then we'll have enough money to buy Mama a box of Valentine's chocolates. Will you do it, Alice, will ya?" He was making excited seal flaps with his hands.

I thought, sure, why not? It might liven Mama up. I talked with Jeffrey, and he tossed me a quarter. Bel thought it was a great idea. I stood out in the hallway while she went into her room to get her black patent leather purse which she kept hidden under the shoe shelf in her closet.

Charlie was already getting dressed to go to the corner store when I gave him the money. I found him standing at the back door struggling with the front zipper of his snow suit. "Oh gosh, no, not this again," he was muttering. I tried to help him, but the zipper wasn't going up or down. "It's okay, Alice. I'll just leave it open," he said.

He was jumping around like he had to pee.

"The wind's gonna come through that, Charlie."

"It's okay. I'll just walk backwards."

He ran out the door and off he flew, down the street to the corner store. A little while later, he came home with the gaudiest heart-shaped box of candies he could find. Purple and orange plastic flowers sat on top of a red heart-shaped box encircled with pink lace. Proud as punch, Charlie stowed the box upstairs in his bedroom and guarded it with such anticipation that before long he had eaten every chocolate that was in it. True to form, it didn't occur to him that he had done anything wrong until we were all waiting downstairs after Valentine's dinner for the big presentation. Suddenly Charlie was in a big muddle, scrambling all over the house looking for glue and cellophane. Nobody knew what he was doing until he brought the deflowered box downstairs. He had covered it in cellophane, and he was clutching the wad underneath like a bouquet. He passed it to Mama as if he truly believed he could carry it off.

"It's from everyone," Charlie announced, proudly sticking out his belly. Mama took the bouquet and shook it next to her ear. "It's awfully light," she said. "I'm sure I won't gain any pounds eating this."

Seeing what Charlie had done, we burst into laughter and jeers.

"Thanks anyway, Charlie," Mama said. Her eyes suddenly filled with tears, and that ended the hilarity.

Later, when I was fixing up in the kitchen, I came across the Valentine on the counter, and irritably called Charlie to come and take it away. Bury it.

One early morning in late March, Jeffrey trotted upstairs looking for Mama. She usually rose at six, and here it was seven-thirty. It was Jeffrey's thirteenth birthday. He knocked softly on her door. No answer. He deliberated a moment, then turned the knob, and poked his head in. The blankets on the bed looked as if they had been spun in a washing machine. The flowered beige wallpaper above the headboard had been scratched to shreds. The paper was flapping off the wall as if Mama had been trying to tear it to pieces.

Jeffrey took a few steps into the room and saw her curled up under a heap of twisted sheets at the foot of the double bed. "Mama?" he whispered. "Mama? Are you awake?" At first, he couldn't account for the red spots in the sheets. He thought they were flowers—poppies or something, and then he saw that it was blood. Mama's face and arms were covered in blood and the sheets had absorbed it like a blotter. Jeffrey took her by the shoulders and shook her. "Mama, wake up! Wake UP!"

I heard him shouting from the kitchen and ran upstairs. Jeffrey was still shaking her. She groaned like a drunken person and her head rolled around like it wasn't attached to her spine. Jeffrey let her go and ran to shut the door just as Bel came flying out of her room. Her dressing gown flapped open and her unhinged breasts were flopping all over the place under her nightie.

"Whatsa matter, whatsa matter?" she cried.

Jeffrey ordered her to call the ambulance. By this time, Charlie and Zack had arrived. They were bashing at one another like two bear cubs, trying to see into the room. Mama had clawed long gashes down her arms and the sides of her body. Her lower lip dangled grotesquely from the corners of her mouth, and it was plain to me that she had bitten clean through the flesh.

After calling the ambulance, I could hear Bel crying on the stairs. "Why did you do that, Madeline? Why?" She got up and disappeared into the bathroom. Zack and Charlie and I huddled around the door of Mama's room. Charlie's eyes were spitting tears as he sucked the back of his hand. "D'ya suppose she's died, Alice, d'ya suppose she's died?" I hugged him and assured him that she would be quite all right, not to worry, but my arms were shaking so bad I thought they'd fall off. Zack went and crouched in the corner of the hallway. He stared at the closed door. He kept shaking his head as if he couldn't knock any sense into it. When the paramedics arrived, I had the presence of mind to shepherd them downstairs and make them breakfast, which nobody ate.

In the Montgomery family, no full explanation has ever been given for this incident. It is never mentioned when the family gathers, although the memory is eternally present in a stitched line that underscores everything that Mama says.

It's strange to say this, but I remember the relief I felt at the time, after the danger had passed. I remember it so well I can smell it in the air, like clean laundry, every spring of my life. During the long months after we moved to Calgary in 1962, Mama had been letting herself die, like a candle flaming out. For reasons I can only dimly appreciate, I think she decided she deserved to die, that she had some kind of penance to pay. So she sealed her windows and doors and let all her demons out in the middle of the night, where they had only her to attack.

It was Bel who arranged for us to spend two mornings a week with Mama in the hospital. She had a private room. The doctors had bandaged her lower face and Mama wore a scarf over the bandage like one of those veiled ladies from Saudi Arabia. We found her new style a bit exotic, but it was her silence and her dead eyes that unsettled us. We worried that when Mama reappeared, she wouldn't be Mama anymore.

After she came home, Bel would read stories to us or to anyone who cared to listen. She chose stories by people like Hermann Hesse that were long and dense but oddly comforting. Mama would sit on the sofa while Jeffrey sat guard beside her, thumbing through comic books. Charlie and I played checkers at the games table, and Zack made log cabins on the floor. None of us said much of anything, but there was a warmth in that living room that stays with me forever. It radiated from Mama's eyes, though they were closed most of the time.

CHAPTER 5

IN THE LIMELIGHT

Fifteen was the year of butterflies, when everything came rushing at me in a high wind. Feelings I'd never experienced before rose and sank into the deep pit of my stomach. Nothing was certain anymore. Before Papa died, I'd been plain headstrong, determined to do whatever I pleased and to hell with the world. I had all the answers and all the best advice, but at fifteen, I lost my authority to menstrual cramps and riptides of inexpressible longing.

To further complicate things, fifteen was also the year that Mama started going out on dates. One evening in May, she emerged from her bedroom wearing a shimmering blue dress with a gold sash and dangly earrings to match. Zack, Charlie, and I were standing in the hallway and we were knocked out by her beauty. She smelled of lavender and roses, and her copper hair was loosely braided into a thick rope that snaked down her back. By this point, her scar had healed over and gave a pout to her lower lip that made her look ravishing.

We all bubbled with questions. Where was she going, all gussied up on that warm spring evening? She held her secret back with a wink, tussled Charlie's hair, and sailed down the stairs, out the front door, and into a cab.

It was about time Mama went out, I thought. Five years was too long to be in mourning over Papa. I headed downstairs to finish the dishes.

Jeffrey was sitting in the kitchen with his best friend Greg Atherton and looking so peeved you'd think Mama was stepping out on *him*. "Where does she think she's going? And who is she going to meet? Why isn't she telling us?" He leaned over the kitchen table and fumed, making Greg feel increasingly uncomfortable. That was unfortunate, because Greg was an attractive guy—one of those strong, silent types who, in my opinion, had years of maturity over Jeffrey. Greg had been trying since before supper to persuade Jeffrey to go out to the school basketball game, and as time ticked on, it looked less and less likely that there'd be any fun in the offing. Oblivious to what anyone else felt, Jeffrey propped himself up on his elbows and tore apart a book of matches as if it were a mouse.

Then Bel came in. Bel always made a point of wearing décolleté sweaters whenever Jeffrey's friends were around. This one was a nauseating lime green with little black roses lining the edges. I don't know what it was about Jeffrey, but he and Aunt Bel always seemed to be in cahoots. Not that they had any rapport, but they were both moody characters and there was a tendency for their moods to intersect. If Bel was in a funk, you could bet that Jeffrey was nearby letting off steam for reasons of his own. I don't think Jeffrey had any particular affection for Bel, and I know he was just as puzzled as I was about why she had dropped her own affairs to set us up in Calgary and pick up the pieces after Papa died. But *something* united those two, and Bel exploited it for all it was worth. She made it clear to the rest of us that if family potential existed at all, it existed in the person of Jeffrey. When she flattered him, Jeffrey would smirk, and his eyes would dart down to her cleavage. Then she'd start flirting, dangling her arms around him. I found those scenes pretty obscene, but they stirred up the butterflies that were hatching in the pit of my stomach.

This time Bel, however, wasn't in any mood for flirting. She didn't say *boo* when she came into the kitchen. She marched straight up to me and demanded, "How long have you been at those dishes, child?"

Then she let me have it. "Where does your mind wander to these days, eh? You've got the cups upside down! You know as well as I do, they should be right side up! Look at this mess...." (This was a constant bone of contention between us. I said the cups would gather dust being right side up. She said the rims would get filthy being upside down. I preferred to know what was at the rim of my glass rather than not know what was crawling around at the bottom.)

She turned to the boys. "You fellows had better get yourselves somewhere else, or this girl will never get her work done."

Jeffrey, who by now had stretched his entire torso across the table, didn't even look up. "We're not bothering her," he said.

"Oh really? You don't think you're bothering her? Look at her. Look, young Mr. Atherton. You've got this poor girl all flustered!"

Damn her to hell. I blushed to my socks, my grimy apron grew maggots, my wide mouth and small breasts and big feet all tried at once to cram themselves into the space under the sink.

Greg looked at me in surprise, as if he hadn't noticed me there before, which was the point, and of course he took his time registering the impression I dreaded.

I squirmed for a whole minute, during which time Bel calmly turned over the cups. Then, when she decided I'd done enough penance, she announced, "All right now, you boys get out of here."

They obliged.

"Why don't *you* get out of here!" I hissed, snapping the dish towel on the counter. "Go back to the hell you came from!"

I ran downstairs to my bedroom which was a mistake

because I heard Jeffrey and Greg in his room. I dashed into my room and scrambled around looking for my running shoes, all set to escape, go somewhere, anywhere.

Then I heard Greg ask, "How old is your sister anyway?" I froze. My heart hammered in my ears.

"Fifteen, goddammit. Listen, Greg, whaddya say you just go to the game yourself. I don't feel like doin' much tonight."

Poor Greg was obviously just trying to make conversation. He must have felt awkward as hell. Jeffrey could do that to people. He could do anything he wanted to people.

But Greg wasn't about to be brushed off so easily. "If you're so pissed off about your mother going out, why don't you go find your own date?"

The door banged and burst open. Greg galloped up the back stairs, two at a time with Jeffrey on his heels. "Come on back here, you coward, and say that to my face!" Jeffrey hollered. The back door slammed. Then it slammed again. A minute later Jeffrey came back in. He was using words we were taught to never utter, like *asshole* and *fucker.*

He went into his room, and I heard him kicking things around. His soccer ball hit the wall a few times along with some shoes and who knows what else. His room was a wreck. Nothing had any protection in there except for his turntable, which he kept on a stool in the closet. Then he went quiet. I heard him go out.

I forgot my injury, along with my running shoes, and wandered back upstairs. I was impressed by Greg. His willingness to stand up to Jeffrey elevated him beyond all other boys in my estimation. I passed through the empty kitchen and into the living room, vaguely thinking that maybe I'd raid the bookshelf for another D.H. Lawrence novel. I only read Lawrence in certain states of mind and then only for the good parts.

Bel was in the living room reading a *Chatelaine* magazine and drinking what appeared to be Scotch from a huge green plastic tumbler. She was slumped in her tattered wingback chair, looking hurt and winded as she flipped distractedly through the magazine.

Now if I had been born a boy, I could have made it through that room with no difficulty whatsoever. An easy matter of grabbing the book and dashing out. The fact was, I never talked to Bel if I could help it. I spied on her a lot, though, which was usually worth its salt in entertainment, if you kept a safe distance away. Bel was a truly fascinating creature, but a dangerous one, a practiced manipulator. Every time you let your defenses down, she'd take it as an invitation to attack. Particularly if you happened to be female, or if she deemed you weren't worth much—which, naturally, was synonymous with being female.

In that moment, though, I felt sorry for her. I thought, Poor Bel is always alone. It didn't occur to me that she ought to be feeling any remorse for her conduct in the kitchen. Just looking at her, hunched over a magazine in that sorry old chair, made me regret what I'd said. I parked myself on the couch adjacent to her and set *The Virgin and the Gypsy* down on the long coffee table in front of me, next to her tumbler.

I figured if I just sat there long enough to be respectable, and if she didn't have anything to say, I could get up and leave in good faith. Well-bred young ladies must remember their manners, even in the presence of people like Bel who do and say exactly what they please, regardless of their listeners or the consequences.

"It's really not necessary for you to stay with me, dear," Bel said. "I'm used to being alone. God knows, that's the way it's always been."

I opened my mouth to apologize for that, along with everything else, but decided against it. She shifted her axis toward me, crossed her legs, and put her chin in her hand. She actually looked attractive in that instant, if you ignored the green sweater and focused instead on her tight black skirt, red pumps, and surprisingly shapely legs. She had sad grey eyes and long black eyelashes that she knew how to flutter.

"Perhaps it's time for me to find my own place to live," she said. "Nobody needs me anymore, certainly not your mother. She's fit as a fiddle now. More fit than ever, I'd say, though she's changed. God knows she's done that a few times in her life. Poor Jon."

She reached for her glass and took a long drink. I

could smell it—Scotch whiskey, and there wasn't much water in it. To my knowledge, Bel wasn't a lush, though she'd accept a highball if anyone offered. Papa used to say that if you left Bel alone over the weekend with a bottle of Scotch, she'd have it polished off by Monday.

"Jon." Papa's name came out mistily. "He was one heck of a handsome man, your father. Irresistible to women. Jeffrey will have some of that in him, you watch."

Bel tipped her glass to me. "Will you get me another one of these, dear?"

"Sure." I got up, went to the cabinet and poured her a couple of fingers from the bottle. I didn't bother going to the kitchen for water. I wondered what was up with Bel. I knew there was a smutty side to her character that longed for male company, but I had never really seen it on display. Not like this. I could have acted offended and made an exit, but she had piqued my curiosity. I wanted to know what she was driving at in her usual reckless fashion, so I handed her the drink and sat down in the passenger seat.

"Is that what brought him and Mama together?" I asked.

She took a gulp and gave me the eye. "You're always around sweeping up the scraps, aren't you, Alice? Well, your Mama ought to be telling you these things. You're old enough to hear. But I don't suppose she'd talk to you like this, would she? No, of course she wouldn't." She yanked at her narrow skirt that was sliding up her thighs.

"Madeline was lucky to land your Papa. Not that she didn't have the looks, but lots of women do. She played her cards right, though she didn't have the faintest idea how to play the game." Bel sniffed condescendingly. "Believe me, your Papa was a catch, if you could keep him. See, Alice, that was the hard part."

I maintained a pretense of detached interest. "So how did she keep him?"

"Let's start with how she got him." Bel thumped her glass down on the side table.

Blood rushed to my cheeks. "What are you implying, Aunt Bel?"

"If you're thinking pregnancy, child, now that just shows how naive you are. Besides, do the math. Of course, she didn't land him with a kid. It was much, much more complicated than that."

She gave me the once-over and reached for her drink. "There are a few things you've got to understand about your mother, Alice. When she was a little girl, she loved the limelight, and everybody adored her. They wound her up, and she sang and danced, and the whole lot of us pampered her to the point of destroying her. She chatted a mile a minute, and spun circles around everyone to please them. She had some talent, I'll give her that, but not an ounce of character. Still, we all thought she'd be a star one day.

"Then, I don't know, somewhere in her mid-teens she just froze up. Nobody knew why. She wouldn't even talk to your Grampa. She went into a depression, locked herself in her room, and refused to go anywhere. Your Grampa couldn't even get her to go to church, and the whole thing nearly worried him into an early grave."

Bel shifted her weight and knocked back her drink like she needed the medicine. "I don't know if you're understanding any of this, Alice, and I'm probably running off at the mouth, but what the hell. I've spent too much of my life not saying a word to anyone. I wish to hell I could write it all down just to get it out of my head."

I didn't know what to say, but I didn't need to say anything because she just plowed on.

"You gotta get this one thing clear, Alice, if you're ever going to understand your mother. She has to have center stage. Even when she went through that depression—and I mean, it was a complete change of personality—she still had to have the limelight."

She leaned over the right arm of her chair so close to me I could smell the Scotch. "I've been watching your Mama all my life. Believe me, I know. She went through this dark period and when she came out of it, she was not the same. She'd developed mysteries. She stopped singing, and as far as I know she never picked it up again. She seemed to be consciously focusing people's attention on her silence. If you looked closely, you could see she had a line of sorrow under her lip. It was there, even before she did that ghastly thing."

Bel straightened up and clicked her tongue as if she had tasted something sour. "It was very alluring, let me tell you. When she was in her late teens, I couldn't take my eyes off her and neither could anyone else. She cultivated the image of a woman deeply bruised at a tender age. She had this look of fear in her eyes. Now I know you haven't the faintest idea what I'm talking about, but it was a look of absolute vulnerability. Like you could take her and crush her and do anything you wanted with her. She brought out the most vicious tendencies in people, and the most tender."

Bel opened her hand. "You know what it's like to hold a baby bird? You're afraid to touch it for fear of breaking its bones, but at the same time you want to crush it in your fist."

Her hand closed. I felt queasy. "I'm not sure I want to hear any more," I said.

She ignored me, determined to stay in the driver's seat. "The reason for your parents' attraction to one another—and I'd say the reason for their problems—was obvious if you just looked at the situation. Your mother made herself appear ravishingly destructible. Like the princess about to fall in the pit. Your father wanted to protect her, but I've got a strong suspicion that there were nights when he just wished he could push her in."

"How do you know all this, Aunt Bel?" I demanded.

"Let's be honest, Alice. What the hell is there in my life that's so exciting? But you're right. It's just the Scotch.

I've got to be an idiot spilling all this out to you, you're nothing but a child. You can't understand any of this."

That did it. I grabbed her empty, greasy tumbler, went to the cabinet and poured her one long, fat drink. "Well, you know, Aunt Bel, you'd be surprised what I've been able to understand. Speaking as one who observes people, I mean."

I wasn't altogether comfortable with that precocious remark, but it made some kind of impression in her muddled head. I handed her the glass and sat down again.

"Well alright, then. How can I put this to you? Your mother became his bird in a cage. He protected her fiercely, and she opened up again. Never sang, to my knowledge, but her old radiance came back. She sparkled at home, and she sparkled in public. Now there was some competition, because like I said, your father was a striking man, and in my view he deserved a lot more of the limelight than he got. Anyway, before you were born, the two of them would go out at night, maybe four or five times a week. Met their friends down in this little Toronto bar on Spadina and did a lot of mixing. Maddy loved it, and Jon would have accepted that if only she'd given him some reassurance that she wouldn't fly the coop. But she never did. It ate at him. You could see the strain growing around his eyes. He was always on edge, and that's where Maddy liked to keep him. The man never got his due. You kids don't know anything about your father, that's proof enough."

92

"We don't know him because he died," I snapped.

She wasn't listening. "All he needed was to know his own worth, and a good woman could have done that for him. But he got caught in her spell, and that was his stupidity. His princess vanished, and he took the fall. That's the real story ... there he was, fine man with backbone who landed in the pit."

Bel's mouth tightened, fishlike, and her eyes teared. Her mind was faraway and I'm sure she even forgot that I was sitting there. "Poor man, poor man," she repeated, dabbing the corner of one eye with a long-nailed finger.

"I remember one night. It was New Year's Eve, and I was visiting. They had a big party. Jon got a real come-on from a strawberry blonde in a peasant dress who was wearing absolutely nothing underneath. His eyes warmed over her body like oil. And I don't mind saying it was damn good to see that side of him after all he put up with."

"I don't really want to—"

"That was New Year's Eve, 1961. Now you put that down in your diary or whatever it is you keep stashed away downstairs in that trunk of yours. There were a lot of hard times for those two after Jeffrey was born. You wonder what held them together. Well, you've still got lots to learn, Alice, but you're not going to get it all out of me tonight."

She swirled the Scotch at the bottom of her glass. I got to my feet, grabbed her glass, and poured her another, lighter one. "You don't know anything about my parents," I said, thrusting the drink at her. "You weren't there."

"You're right, dear. Of course, I know nothing." Her tone was snarky. "I stayed out of your parents' lives most of the time. I had to. It was too hard." She kicked off her shoes.

"What are you saying?"

"Your Papa loved your Mama too much. You understand? It wasn't healthy. He resented her until it became a sickness, and why shouldn't he have had a little tending to himself? Maddy was always coaxing him, driving him crazy to go hither and yon, anywhere to get out. It's a wonder she had any babies at all. She didn't want any damn babies, but she didn't have the character to say so."

A sharp pang of emptiness ran through me. The words "damn babies" went round and round, enlarging the void in my chest. I sat back down on the couch and listened numbly while she babbled on.

"I'll tell you something else, Alice. Just after you were born, your Mama decided she'd had enough mothering for a while. She wanted to get away for a couple of weeks. Jon was reluctant, but he agreed to it. She made arrangements to go visit a friend in Montreal. He booked her reservations and brought the babysitter in to stay for a few days. You won't remember Elaine, but she was their *au pair* for a few years. Nice looking girl, too, from Le Havre.

"Your Mama was really excited about going away, and

I expect that hurt your Papa even more. Anyway, when he drove her to the airport, he took his time. Stopped for gas and drove behind all the old folks and took all the busiest streets. Madeline was chatting up a storm the whole way, so geared up she didn't notice a thing. Jon just kept driving, calm as a clam, drove and drove in an enormous circle, and ended up right back home.

"Well, I'll tell you, if that had been me instead of your mother, I would have been asking myself some questions. Like who is this man I've been living with all these years? Why would he do this? What's in his heart? But not your Mama, oh no, and this was the clincher. She just got out of the car and headed for the front door. Never said a word, just continued about her business. Madeline's elusive, let me tell you. After that, your father started holding less back. He'd go out of his way to do things that should have hurt her, but they had no effect whatsoever. That's when it dawned on him that he was completely alone, in love with nothing and loved by no one. Your Mama's incapable of love, and that's a fact. No wonder the poor man's heart attacked him. It attacked him all right.… What a waste."

She clawed at her forehead and slouched into her armchair like a sack of seeds. I hated her with a passion and concentrated on the tumbler that she dangled precariously over the rug. When it dropped, I'd be free.

She jolted up and slammed her glass on the coffee table. Pulled her skirt down and primped the back of

95

her perm. "I've gotta go to bed, dammit," she muttered. "What a disaster, what a disaster!" She pushed herself off the chair, got to her feet, and started wobbling around the room.

I retrieved her shoes from under the coffee table, and as I stood up, I saw Jeffrey's shadow move on the dining room wall. He'd been standing in the kitchen for I don't know how long. Bel turned on me. "Your mother's got no right to saunter out of here with whomever she pleases. Do you have any idea who she went out with tonight? Eh? No, of course you don't. Well, I'll tell you. She's running around with a boy no older than Jeffrey. He's a model. Lies on a plank stark naked so that so-called artists can leer at his anatomy."

I laughed out loud. "Is that so wrong?"

She pushed me out of her way. "This is the last straw. Who's going to protect your father's memory?"

"He's been dead for five years!"

"Five years is only a long time for a child," she slurred. "Jeffrey understands that. Your mother's got her nerve. I don't know what's happening to her, but I don't like it. Her softness is gone. She's becoming hard. I've seen it before. I'll be gone in a week, you watch. Mark my words."

With that warning, she shuffled upstairs to bed and I was left standing in the dark, holding her shoes.

CHAPTER 6

HOLY SMOKES

"Remove yourself from this room, Alice!" Aunt Bel drummed her long finger on the breakfast table and glared at me with her crow's eyes. She was dressed as if she meant to go to war in a khaki shirt and maroon pants.

I took two steps backward and kept my eyes on Mama who was sitting adjacent to Bel at the table. "I only answer to Mama."

"Did you hear what I said, child?"

"Shut up, Isabel," Mama snapped. "Alice, you're fifteen. In my books that's old enough to hear what you want to hear. I haven't got any secrets."

Mama leaned back and crossed her bare legs, revealing the lacy edge of her slip under a jade dressing gown.

"Come on, Isabel. Let's have it out."

"Don't you start accusing me of anything, Madeline. You're the one running around with a kid twenty years younger than yourself. What do you think you're doing to your children's minds with all that hanky-panky? So, don't you talk back to me, Missy."

Bel slapped her thighs and stood up from the table like an army general. Mama rose with her, cinching her dressing gown, while I stepped into the shadows on the other side of the refrigerator.

"So it's a battle you want is it, Isabel? Fine. Well, then, I know exactly what you've been up to lately. You might be sneaky, but you leave a pretty good trail." They faced one another, eye to eye.

"I think you're coming undone again, Madeline. Setting yourself up for another nervous breakdown. Ever since Jon died, it's been one thing after another. Don't try and deny it, it's obvious from the art in your bedroom. That disgusting crap couldn't be sold in a junk store."

"That's it." Mama grabbed a pottery pitcher from the counter and hurled it at Bel. It grazed her on the cheek and shattered on the wall behind her. Bel yelped and stumbled backward. I thought she might topple, but she recovered. "You're cruel, Madeline," she whimpered. "And now you're proving to be nothing but a whore."

Mama laughed. "Golly, that's rich. Who's the whore, Bel? Do you really think that my children don't talk to me? You think that they would go to you before they'd come to me? You may be lots of things, but you're not discreet."

"I have no idea what you're talking about." Bel fluffed her dyed black hair and went to the sink. She tore a paper towel from the roll and ran it under cold water. Patting her bruised cheek as though she were tending to a baby, she looked tearfully out the window.

Mama didn't appear to notice the histrionics. Instead she took a nail file out of her dressing gown pocket and started shaping her nails. "The way I hear it, Isabel, you've gained a little weight in the region of your chest."

Bel frowned. She wasn't prepared for Mama's tactics.

"I never would have thought your buxom figure could turn anyone off. Especially a nice strapping young man just reaching his prime. It was quite a reveal, by all accounts. Golly, you almost got his pants off. What on earth went wrong?"

Bel spun around. "Who's been feeding you lies? And where do you get the nerve to say those dirty things in the presence of that child?" She meant me, of course, standing on the other side of the fridge.

"Guess he just got so excited in the face of all that woman flesh that he plumb wound himself down," Mama continued, enjoying herself tremendously.

"I won't have you speaking to me this way!" Bel shouted, throwing her arms in the air. "Whatever Jeffrey told you was a half-truth. He's always trying to protect you, just like his father did. Treats you like you were made of glass, poor deluded child. Now, are you ready to hear the facts?" She planted her hands on her hips. "I'm not denying anything."

Mama smiled at her fiercely, eyes blazing. "Go on, Isabel."

"What do you expect is going to happen when you go off galivanting with young boys? What do you think your own kids are learning?" She stomped over to me and grabbed me by the shoulder of my T-shirt. "They're gonna learn, one way or the other. Might as well be me teaching them what their Mama's out there doing."

Mama pulled me away from her. She stood behind me and placed her hand over my heart in a manner that claimed me as her own. "So, this is your form of revenge is it, Isabel? Do you have plans to initiate all my children?"

"I'm not interested in your children. They can all go to hell as far as I'm concerned." With that, Bel marched out of the kitchen.

I spun around, looked at Mama with big eyes, and slapped my hand over my mouth. We burst out laughing.

"I'd say it's time Aunt Bel hit the road, eh, Alice?"

"High time," I said. Mama went and got the broom out of the closet and started to sweep up the shards of pottery. She didn't look up. She just kept on sweeping briskly, as if she meant to whisk all the demons out of the house.

Back in the safety of my bedroom, I thought about what I had overheard. Jeffrey had just turned seventeen. Was it possible that Bel could've tried *that*? Anything was possible with Bel. Holy smokes.

Mama was grabbing control visibly, almost by the

hour. Bel had maintained possession of the household for five years, ever since Papa's death. You couldn't go to the bathroom without her knowing what you did in there. The fact that Mama was working all the time left the whole territory unguarded, and Bel had taken full advantage of it. She bossed us four kids around, playing one off the other until no one could possibly identify the culprit in any disagreement. She took a dislike to Charlie and probably did the most damage to him, because nobody trusted Charlie anymore. Whenever some trivial matter arose that gave Bel the opportunity to inflict punishment, she'd say that it was Charlie who had told her. Poor Charlie would go into a tantrum, roar his way through the house like a lunatic, and go off somewhere to cry. As far as Jeffrey, Zack, and I were concerned, the mania was clear evidence of Charlie's guilt. No one ever thought to question Bel. Now that I'm older, I have to wonder if Charlie really was the snitch. Not that Charlie didn't have it in him to start wars and then stand around looking angelic while the rest of us took the flak. But Bel could spot a weakness in character and use it to destroy you. It was the best weapon she had, and she had used it on Mama for years.

Now Madeline was staging a comeback. She'd started painting again, and though Bel might have appeared to support her artistic endeavors, she had always been threatened by her sister's creativity. Mama hadn't opened a paint box since the move to Calgary. But after working for more than three years as office manager for Rex Harding Advertising, she got promoted to the graphics department. No one at work knew she had any talent until Lisa, one of the account managers, became a personal friend. Lisa saw a few of Mama's old sketches and brought them to the attention of Mr. Harding, who asked to see her portfolio. Mama brought in a few water-colors that she'd done in art college, and Mr. Harding promoted her on the spot. For Mama it was a red-letter day. She couldn't believe that her skills merited notice of any kind, much less from someone so prominent. She quit her evening job and resumed her art with zeal.

She stripped the curtains from her bedroom window, replaced them with blinds, and set up her art table where it could catch the sun. At first, she didn't seem to care what emerged, and the result was dizzying. So far as I know, Mama had never done abstracts before, but there they were. Mad swirls of color, lines, circles, and cubes on huge sheets of newsprint, each one quickly taped to her bedroom walls, as if she barely had the time to hang what she finished before she started the next painting. Her bedroom became an angry, passionate storm of red and orange shapes, while Mama herself grew more chipper by the day. Then in February she started going to a night class at the university, which was where the nudes orig-inated. I'd go upstairs to her bedroom sometimes when she was out, and just stare at the anatomy. It beat doing French. It even beat writing for a while. It wasn't enough for Mama to draw a lone, reclined nude. She preferred orgies of bodies. Her "studies" gave you a feeling that there wasn't room enough for all that energy on the paper, that if they were released from the confines of the page, they would burst apart and consume all the available space. The back pages of my notebooks were filled with awkward attempts to recall regions of the anatomy that so completely intoxicated me it was all I could do to remain rooted to the ground.

The resurgence of Mama's art heralded the start of the Montgomery family's first major global war. It was a battle of territories that had been building since the beginning of time.

It seemed to me that Bel was one of those unfortunate characters who yearned to live in the middle of anybody's story but her own. Maybe she thought her own story wasn't worth beans. It couldn't have been easy for Bel to have seen her mother carted off to an institution when she was only seven years old. I have the impression that after her mother left, her father didn't know what to do with her. He was a drinker and, as Grandma Mabel once said, Gerald couldn't sleep with that. He wrote to Bel's father to suggest that young Isabel come east by train.

I asked her about her journey once when we'd gone to the mountains for a picnic. I was about twelve and Bel had driven us up to Lake Minnewanka in her station wagon. We were wandering around, looking at mountain sheep, and Bel was taking pictures with her new polaroid camera.

"I guess you didn't have a camera on that train trip you took across the country," I said in an offhand way.

"Of course not." She peered at the picture coming into view.

"Did you travel all by yourself? I'd be too scared to ride a train across the country, even at my age."

"It was an adventure," she said.

"How so?"

"There were nice people on the train. An older English gentleman and his wife gave me a Cornish pasty. Look at that ram. Isn't he magnificent? I had their address in England. I figured if Uncle Gerald and Aunt Mabel didn't work out, I could go to Yorkshire." Under her breath she said, "Sometimes I wish I had."

She was wearing an Australian outback hat with a string under the chin that kept cutting off her view of the photograph.

"But what was the train ride like?"

"Just lovely, dear. Didn't I just say that?" She threw an arm around my shoulders. "Let me tell you, Alice in Wonderland, there is nothing, absolutely nothing interesting about my life. You're barking up the wrong tree." There was a chill in her voice that felt vaguely like a threat, so I backed off.

In the theatre of life, Bel insisted on being a member of the audience. Madeline was the star, hogging the spotlight. She snagged the leading man, the one that

Bel would have liked to have had for herself. It must have satisfied her to think that Mama had all but assassinated her husband. Then, after he died, she could swoop in, take Mama under her wing, and keep her there until she suffocated.

She hadn't counted on resistance, though, and for the first four years, there was no reason to think she would get any. But the resurgence of Mama's art signaled that she was making a strong recovery and maybe even staging a coup.

Bel wasn't about to let her sister's little victory in the kitchen go unchallenged. Mama had four obvious areas of vulnerability. Already Bel had managed to get to me, Charlie, and Jeffrey. Now she was circling her last and most fatal target—Zack. Ten years old and the youngest in the Montgomery family, Zack knew nothing about his origins. Bel swooped in on him, that very afternoon.

"I know, baby," she whispered, rocking Zack back and forth on his twin bed by the window. He was clutching a piece of paper. "Now don't you go telling your mother. She doesn't know that your father wrote me that letter. And you can be sure nobody else knows about all this business except you and me and your Mama."

"Mama shoulda told me." Zack was sobbing.

"C'mon now," said Bel a little impatiently. "Let's dry those tears. You're a grown man now."

Zack let her clean up his face with her Kleenex. "But why did Papa do that, Aunt Bel? How come?"

"You get a little older, Zack, and then you ask me that question again. I'll tell you what I know. Meanwhile you hide that letter, and don't you dare breathe a word. Your Mama will be back soon. I'm going over to Uncle Ro's place for the night, so you just clean yourself up and tuck that letter away."

She got up and left him sitting on his twin bed next to Charlie's, holding a letter from his Papa that had lodged like a bullet in his heart.

Charlie scrambled out from underneath his bed. "Boy, Aunt Bel's gonna get it this time," he shrieked, stomping out of the room. Zack dashed to the door and halted him. "You don't know what's going on, Charlie. So just don't you dare open your big mouth."

Charlie stuck his hands in his pockets and pushed out his belly. "Oh yeah? I sure do know, Zack. *Everybody* knows."

Zack clenched his fist in Charlie's face. "You dunno nothin'."

"Yes I do. I know 'cause Alice told Jeffrey an' me the whole story."

Zack's hand fell limp. Charlie squirmed past him and galumphed out into the hall. Then Zack shut the door with a click and, as methodically as he did everything, he went to the night table, drew out a box of matches, struck one, and set his bed on fire. He tossed the letter into the flames along with Dolly, the little crocheted doll that had been with him since his birth.

Jeffrey smelled the smoke, charged upstairs, and dragged Zack out the room. Then he called the fire department. By the time the firemen had put out the blaze, Zack and Charlie's room was completely gutted.

When Mama arrived home from work, we were huddled in the living room, all except Zack. He didn't return until later on that night, and when he did, he went into the kitchen and made himself a baloney sandwich as if it were just another ordinary day. He sat down at the table and had started to eat when Mama burst into the kitchen.

"What on earth happened today?" she demanded.

He shrugged, looked up at her with his hard eyes, and kept chomping.

Mama swung at the sandwich and it went flying. Then she grabbed him by the shoulder of his blue denim shirt and marched him upstairs to the burnt bedroom. "What's this all about, Zack?"

"It don't matter anyway, Mama," he said. His tone was cold.

"What do you mean it doesn't matter? Are you out of your mind? Do you need psychiatric help or something? What in God's name provoked this?"

"Charlie musta told you."

Mama looked confused. "Charlie? What's he got to do with it?"

"He was under the bed when Aunt Bel told me. *You*

should know." He glared at Mama with bitter accusation.

Mama took him by the shoulders and shook him hard. "Know what?"

"Nobody *told* me." He held his tears back in a pout. Standing in the doorway, I hoped that he would just let all that grief out. Let Mama take him into her arms. But Zack was too proud, and Mama lost her patience. She launched into a tirade about the bills and the fire insurance that had expired and the lovely antique dresser that was the only thing she brought from Toronto because it belonged to Grampa.

"It was a letter from PAPA!" Zack screamed. "He wrote it to Aunt Bel, but it was about me, so she gave it to me. It's not like you don't already know!"

Mama became calm suddenly, calm as a breeze.

"And did Papa say you were adopted?"

"Yes."

"And did Papa say that he was your father?"

"Yes."

"And I am not your mother."

"That's correct." His eyes could have burned holes through flesh.

"That's what made you start this fire?"

"Nobody *told* me."

Mama charged out of the room and went straight to the bank where she depleted her savings account to pay the deposit that Bel had put down on the house. She wrote Bel a certified cheque. Then she picked up the phone book and made a dozen calls before she finally got hold of a company that could get the move done before Bel came home the next day.

Mama didn't say a word, and it sure wasn't in my nature to blow the horn. I couldn't sleep a wink that night. Zack and Charlie were huddled in sleeping bags on the living room floor. Charlie worried that the fire was proof of his demonic influence on Zack. He spent the whole night telling Zack over and over that he hadn't breathed a word to Mama, really and truly he hadn't, when all the while Zack knew he hadn't and it was irrelevant. But he wasn't in the mood to put out Charlie's fire, so he just lay on the floor all night long, staring at the ceiling and listening to Charlie whine. That would have been punishment enough.

Bel must have come home in the middle of the night because she was asleep at five-thirty in the morning when the movers arrived. Two hefty men came to the door and Mama sailed downstairs like a ghost. She turned on the porch lights, and she had the door open before they could ring the bell. "Don't worry about the kitchen," she whispered. "Just take the stuff in the dining room and the living room. I'll be glad to get rid of this junk. I can tell you it's a bloody disgrace."

"It's all going to this address, Mrs. Montgomery?"

"Yes. There are a few things that will stay. I'll show you. Don't take that lamp...."

And on it went until six. The movers were light on

their feet. I don't know if Mama had told them to go quietly, but they did. Zack and Charlie woke up as the world around them started to whirl. They stood in a daze, both of them in their red striped pajamas, watching the magic act of the disappearing living room.

When the downstairs furniture had been removed and the movers were heading upstairs to Mama's room, Bel woke. She burst into the hall, and she was sticking her lower denture into her mouth when she ran smack into one of the movers. "Robbers!" she screamed, rushing back into her room. "Robbers!"

The men shrugged her off as a lunatic and continued down the hall to Mama's bedroom where they had a couple of chairs to pick up. Bel grabbed a big glazed vase full of plastic flowers and charged the man in the rear. She whacked him on the back, and he dropped to the floor.

The other man started roaring obscenities, and Mama came sprinting upstairs with me, Charlie, and Zack on her heels. Jeffrey heard the commotion from the basement, and he was part way up the stairs when Mama confronted Bel. She shoved the cheque into her bosom and declared, "This is my house now, Bel. You're moving out!"

"I'm doing no such thing," Bel said.

Jeffrey ran to the top of the stairs and stood between them. "Mama said get out, and that means now, Bel."

"What's happened? I don't understand. Why are

these people in the house?" Bel backed into the shadows, clutching the cheque and fiddling with her loose dentures as the two men made their way downstairs.

"Your stuff is going to Roland's house unless you want me to redirect it," said Mama.

"Why? Why are you pushing me out?"

"Zack burned his room down," said Jeffrey. "Can't you smell it?" Mama started down the stairs and Jeffrey followed, but when she got to the kitchen she turned around and stopped him. "Thanks, Jeffrey, but I don't need you to stand guard for me anymore. Just leave me alone."

Bel stumbled back to her room, using the handrail for support. The men left the house quietly and drove off in the moving van with most of Bel's stuff.

Half an hour later, Bel emerged from her room dressed in a burgundy coat and a black feathery hat. She clutched her patent leather purse, which I assumed held the certified cheque and, with an injured dignity that I'd never before witnessed, she glided down the stairs and out the front door.

At dinner time, the moving van returned to the house, followed by a white Studebaker. A slim man in a polo shirt rang the doorbell, and I answered it. He said, "Hello, you must be Alice. I'm Bel's friend, Roland. I wonder if I might speak with your mother."

He was well spoken and handsome, with rusty hair and freckles. I'd guess he was somewhere in his forties. I went upstairs to get Mama, and she came down wearing a white smock with colored paint spattered all over it. She went out to the porch, shut the front door, and had a little chat with Roland. I couldn't hear what they were saying, but after a few minutes Mama seemed at ease. Through the sidelight, I could see that they were both laughing.

"What happened?" I asked when she came inside.

"Apparently, Ro doesn't want the furniture. He's not saying he doesn't want Bel, though. I guess they'll have to work it out."

By four in the afternoon, all Bel's belongings had been returned and were stacked in a heap in the middle of the living room. It was like looking at Bel's life. Nothing but a pile of junk.

I remember feeling sad, thinking about Bel. She spent so much time interfering in our lives. Did she have nothing invested in her own? The war had ended, or so I thought. Bel had come back, and she was with Mama in her bedroom. They were speaking in hushed tones, and working it out, I assumed. Like a good reporter, I figured I had enough of the story to file.

I went to my bedroom in the basement, sat at my desk, and made quick notes in my journal, pressed by some imaginary deadline. Suddenly my door banged open, and Jeffrey strode in.

"Hey!" I cried.

"Look, Alice, I've got to talk to you about something."

"I already know what you've got to say, Jeffrey." I was trying to concentrate, and his intrusion annoyed me, to say the least.

He sat on my bed. "What do you know?"

I spun around on my chair. "I know Bel probably tried to seduce you, and you probably let her."

He gave me a murderous look. "It's no business of yours."

"Look, Jeffrey, you burst in on me. And I'm busy."

He stood up and went to the door. "Forget it, Alice. Forget I tried to say anything. Just stay up there on your little cloud."

"What are you saying, Jeffrey?" I threw my journal on the bed out of pure frustration.

"I'm saying that you spend all your time scribbling fiction in those notebooks, and you haven't got a clue what's really going on. I'm telling you, if you want facts, you have to go to Aunt Bel."

"Is that so." I snorted.

"Mama tells us nothing. I think she's been lying to us all along."

"You've got a real reliable source there, Jeffrey. Aunt Bel is a rat, and you lowered yourself to do whatever the heck you did with her in her dirty little nest. What kind of information did you get from her? Hope it was good because you sure paid a high price for it. Why did you come in here, anyway?"

He sighed, leaned on the doorframe and looked at

the floor. "I didn't come to fight, Alice. I came here to explain something to you. I didn't get any more information from Bel than I already knew. And she didn't seduce me, either. The whole thing was sick. But Bel knows a whole lot more about this family than we do. How come no one around here ever asks the real question?"

I crossed my arms to fend off whatever evil might be coming my way. "And what would that be."

"How *did* Papa die, exactly? Do you know? I don't believe Mama anymore. Why doesn't she tell us the truth?"

"Papa's death is too painful to talk about, Jeffrey. You know that."

"Is it? Really? Are we afraid to hurt her, or does she just not care? Maybe she's just too damn busy!" He kicked the doorframe. "While you're working it all out there, why don't you try answering that?" He left, pounding a wall as he stomped down the hall.

Jeffrey, I decided, belonged to the other camp. Bel had poisoned him, just like she'd poisoned Charlie. I carried on with what I was doing and erased the whole thing from my mind.

According to Charlie, Bel and Mama's conversation went on well into the night, and Bel did a lot of crying. He couldn't hear the words, but it sounded to him like Bel was begging to stay. Next morning Mama came downstairs looking as though she'd been in a boxing match. But it was Bel who came out the loser.

She moved out a few days later. She lived in a basement apartment in northeast Calgary and kept seeing Ro until he finally agreed to let her move into his big house in Mount Royal. The relationship didn't last. The way I understand it, Roland started seeing some mystery woman, and after a couple of months, he confronted Bel with the news that he'd fallen head over heels. Bel moved out again and went to live outside the city, in Okotoks, where she resumed teaching elementary school.

Sometimes I think that the mystery woman was Mama having a lark, but that would be fiction, and I'm doing my best to stick to the facts.

CHAPTER 7

SEEKING PAPA

I've never been able to understand dreams. Sometimes they stay with you in the morning as if they're beached, and you have to wait for the tide to come in and sweep them away. In my experience, when they get beached, they're something big. Sometimes too big to return to the sea. They just grow legs and walk into the day.

I can't remember ever dreaming about Papa, but I did last night. I had a sick feeling that I'd kept him waiting for a long time. I was running through an underground cave, searching for him. There were many rooms, crammed full of people, but after I had raced through them all, I ended up back where I started. I kept trying to recall Papa's bristled face, the baffled expression in his eyes. I expected that if I found him, he would likely be alone, taking it all in from the sidelines, dragging on a cigarette and wondering why everybody was making such a big to-do about nothing.

I chased my image of Papa round and round until I thought I was going to be suffocated in the crush. The place began to look more and more unfamiliar. I called out to him in a panic. But instead of Papa, a cadre of young men answered my call. They were all eager to help me find him. "What does he look like, exactly?" one of them asked. I tried to answer, but I couldn't pry my jaws open to get the words out. The harder I tried, the more they clamped down. Then, as abruptly as it began, the dream dissolved. I can still see the perplexed expressions in the young men's eyes and feel the rising shame of being where I didn't belong, looking for someone I would never find.

Two days after Papa died, Jeffrey took five-year-old Zack out to the parking lot of the funeral home and gave him a lesson in playing catch with a softball. Charlie and I stayed in the parlor with Mama and Bel. It was a toss-up which of my two parents was more dead. Papa lay on one side of the room in a mahogany box. Mama lay on the other side on a chaise lounge. The glow in her complexion was gone, and her face was the color of chalk. She had shoved all her beautiful hair up under a black turban. When visitors arrived, Bel would wrestle Mama up and she would get to her feet, rocking on her heels like a doll. Bel greeted them all with perfume sweet enough to make you sick, and after a few uncomfortable moments, the people would leave. Then Mama would collapse again. It went on like that for three days.

None of us kids owned anything black. Bel, who flew in from Calgary to see to Mama's affairs, ignored the fact that Jeffrey and Zack didn't follow custom to the rule. That in itself was remarkable, because Bel was a real stickler when it came to appearances. I guess she had too many things on her mind, so she only nagged me. Grudgingly, I found some old black tights and a hideous skirt downstairs in the storage closet. The stockings were too small, and the lace skirt was made for some old woman in the Edwardian era. It fit me okay at the waist, but the hips had to be pinned in about half a foot on each side. The worst of it was that it gathered electricity at the calves and cinched my legs together so I didn't have much choice but to sit still. Charlie always honored custom, and so without saying anything he dug up some old trousers that were handed down from Jeffrey. He couldn't hold them up with his little waist, so Bel strapped him into some suspenders that threatened to damage him for life.

True to nature, Charlie stayed close to Mama the entire time, like her personal angel. He knelt at the foot of the chaise and stared at her as if she were some sort of religious idol. If she wanted water or food, Charlie would pop up, fetch it, and return to the place where he had stationed himself. He stayed there for the entire first day, and for a good part of the second, too.

Jeffrey didn't want to go the funeral home after the first day. Bel let him and Zack stay home to do what they pleased. Nobody asked any questions.

I wasn't keen on the idea of hanging around the funeral parlor, but I didn't want to make any waves. Bel would have resisted the idea of letting me go home: first, because I was a girl; and second, because she wanted to show everybody that she had a loving niece. Nevertheless, I stayed on because I chose to. It wouldn't have mattered to Mama, one way or the other, but I felt I needed to sit in that straight-backed chair and wait. Wait for what, I don't know, but I couldn't take my eyes off that polished mahogany box. When the rare visitor passed by it and lifted the lid, my heart raced. Maybe if it had been nailed shut, I could have gone home.

Time passed. I remember a clock ticking on the unused fireplace mantle, measuring empty minutes and hours of silence while Mama slept and Bel paced back and forth.

At some point in the afternoon of the second day, Charlie started to fidget. He blinked his eyes and scratched his nose and frowned anxiously at Mama. Then he shook her leg. Nothing. He shook it again more vigorously. No sign of life. He got to his feet and started pulling violently at his crotch—poor Charlie, he must have been sore. Then he stopped suddenly. He stared at Papa's casket as if he had just noticed it was there.

Bel had left the room. Charlie rubbed his chin

thoughtfully and looked back at Mama, then at the box. He scrambled over to me and tugged at my hand. "C'mon, Alice. Let's see if Papa is really inside there."

My heart pounded. It was a horrible idea, and one that had been occurring to me regularly for nearly two days.

"Of course, he's inside there, Charlie. Come here and let me fix those braces before you hang yourself."

He stepped back from me and would not be put off. "Is he really in there, Alice?" he asked, holding my gaze with all the intensity he could muster.

"C'mon, Charlie. Forget it now, would you? Aunt Bel's gonna be back here any minute."

"No, Alice. 'Cause if he's in there, he might still be alive."

"Charlie, you're crazy. Now get over here so I can adjust those suspenders."

He stomped off to the end of the room where the coffin stood, and then he stomped back. "How are we going to know he isn't alive if we don't look inside? What if he is and he can't breathe in there?"

Now the problem was tempting because the fact of the matter was that neither of us had any proof that Papa had actually died. Charlie, in his own crazy way, was right. Papa had gone off to work just like usual. He'd already had one heart attack the year before, but he had recovered. Come to think of it, it was Bel who had delivered the bad news. She flew to Toronto the next day and she was doing the supper dishes when she announced to us that our Papa had died. With a few words spoken over running water she turned us into orphans, banished from the center of the universe.

So, it occurred to me, why should we believe Bel when she wasn't around most of the time, anyway? Maybe the whole thing was staged. Maybe Mama and Papa and Bel were in league to get rid of us, farm us off to some foster home or something.... It wasn't likely, but we had to make sure. We didn't have much time. I could hear Bel down the hall, whispering to the undertaker. Their voices were becoming more audible. Charlie pulled me to my feet, and we scrambled over to the casket. We lifted the lid together, one, two, three. I didn't get a very good view because I took one look, ducked my head behind Charlie's back, and squeezed my eyes shut. But Charlie opened the lid all the way up and took everything in.

"Bel's coming!" I cried, tugging at him. "Shut the lid, Charlie. Hurry!"

Charlie froze. I reached up from behind him, grabbed the cover, and yanked it down. I was dizzy and sick to my stomach. Charlie put his hand over his mouth and turned around to face me.

"He's not *in* there," he whispered.

"Charlie, I'm gonna be sick. Stop it."

"That's not Papa. He's not *in* there, Alice. That's just a *dummy*."

I couldn't breathe. I ran flat out into Bel on my way through the door and threw up all over her. The hullabaloo that followed even woke up Mama. Charlie went berserk. He threw himself on the undertaker and started hollering, "Where'd you hide my Papa? Where is he?" The undertaker, a round man with spectacles, tried to wrestle him down, but Charlie thrashed and pounded on his chest until the only one who could stop him was Mama. She took him into her arms on the floor and, poor Charlie, he bawled and bawled until the undertaker finally drove the whole lot of us home.

A few weeks after the funeral, Bel announced that we needed to have a family meeting. Everybody piled into the library where all the important family gatherings were held. Mama sat on the love seat wearing a pair of old blue jeans and a long white shirt that had belonged to Papa. She hadn't washed her hair for a while, and it sat limp on her shoulders as if it were mourning too. Jeffrey and Charlie took the easy chairs, though there was nothing easy about the way Charlie sat. He kept pulling on the suspenders that Bel insisted he wear to keep his pants up. I sat on the carpeted floor with Zack who instinctively crawled under my arm for protection. Bel got herself a straight-backed chair from the dining room, and she placed it in front of the fireplace. She sat down primly with a notebook, in which she'd itemized "Things to Do". Then she began her speech.

"Your mother and I have reviewed the family finances." She cleared her throat and peered at us over her bifocals. "I'm afraid it is not going to be possible for your mother to make the payments on the house, and your father, I'm afraid, had a bit of debt." She glanced at Mama who slumped and fiddled with a button on her shirt as if she were one of us. "My recommendation to you is that the family move to Calgary, where I live. It's very pretty there, with mountains and lakes, the clearest lakes in the world. You can ski and camp and have all sorts of fun, while still having access to all the amenities of the city."

I thought, if that's the way she talks to her elementary school children, she's probably not the most popular teacher.

"Do we have to change schools?" Jeffrey asked.

"Yes, but we're not going to even think about moving until after the school year ends," Mama said. It sounded like she didn't want to move at all.

"I'll do all the work of finding a good home for everybody to live in," said Bel. "I know all the best neighborhoods in the city, and I've got a bit of money tucked away that will serve as a down payment. You're dealing with enough as it is. You don't have to worry about how you'll come through to the other side. Just trust me. Everything will work out fine. Any questions?"

"What about Papa?" Charlie asked. "Is he coming too?"

Bel flew back to Calgary in June. By then Mama had revived a little, only because she had to. Slowly boxes of clothing and books piled up, and Mama's watercolor paintings disappeared from the walls. She dismantled her studio on the third floor with the help of friends who came and went, taking all her art materials away. Removal trucks parked on the street, and men carried out furniture and boxes of things that Mama either sold to the secondhand store on Queen Street or gave to the Good Samaritans. The magic blue Persian carpet in the library got rolled up and carted away. When nothing remained but the essentials, as Mama called them, the junk truck came and took all the bits and pieces away: toys we'd discarded, dishes we didn't use, old chairs, stools, tables, tattered books, and clothing. Mama put a big junk box in each one of our rooms and ordered us to fill it. I dumped almost everything in mine to please Mama, including my collection of dolls and all their clothing. I had four sister dolls that weren't happy about turning into trash, but I stopped my ears to their protests. I was ten years old and, as Bel had said, it was time to grow up.

During the move, Grampa drove in from Cobourg to spend a week or two with Mama and help her with the packing. Mama's father was a gentle, slight old man of seventy-one, and he'd been alone for over five years. Mama wouldn't let him do much more than make tea.

When Sunday morning came round, Grampa got all dressed up to go to church. He sat at the kitchen table and quietly listened to the radio while he waited for Mama to come downstairs. He waited until half past twelve, and by then it was too late to go. Mama eventually appeared with an armload of old clothes that she intended to give away. She took one look at Grampa, dumped the clothes, and shut the radio off. "Papa, listen to me," she said. She sat down beside him, taking his freckled hand in hers. "I love you, but I'm not able to go to church anymore."

"His death is not your fault, Madeline," he said softly.

Mama swallowed hard. "I don't know about that. All I know is that I'm going to miss all the time I didn't spend with him."

Tears welled up in Grampa's eyes, and he withdrew his hand gently, nodding his head up and down. He didn't stay to the following Sunday. I guess he figured there wasn't much he could do to help Mama.

As spring turned into summer, we had all come to accept the inevitable move. All except Charlie. Charlie was a real problem that summer. He had got it into his head that Papa was still alive somewhere, and Mama couldn't talk any sense into him at all. Even Grampa tried, and who wouldn't listen to Grampa? Well, Charlie wouldn't. He was as hardheaded as a goat and determined to find Papa—so determined that a few days after Grampa's visit, Charlie disappeared. Mama found his drawers ransacked for T-shirts, which were all he put into his suitcase. No trousers, no underwear. Just T-shirts. And off he went.

By that point, the house had been sold and all but

the bare essentials had been packed up and sealed into cartons. The fact that Mama had been trying so hard to persuade Charlie that Papa was dead, and we had to move on, was good therapy for her. She had started to absorb the catastrophic fact. But when Charlie ran away, Mama nearly collapsed again. It was ten o'clock on a Wednesday evening when Jeffrey called the police. Mama hovered around him, wrapped in a shawl and shaking uncontrollably. The police arrived and Jeffrey went off with them. He didn't come back until after midnight. Mama rushed him at the front door and grabbed him by the sleeves as if to plead Charlie out of him. But there was no sign of Charlie.

On Thursday the police filed a story with the newspapers and Charlie's picture appeared on the front page. It wasn't until Friday night that the phone rang. It was St. Joseph's hospital. Charlie had been hit by a car. He'd stepped out in front of a van on Queen Street, and there wasn't a thing the driver could do. Charlie was in a delirium when it happened. He hadn't eaten for three days. His face was bruised, and he had cracked a couple of ribs, but other than that he was whole.

We all went down to the hospital to see him. Mama and I went in first. She couldn't take more distress, and Charlie should have been able to realize that, but he was possessed by the idea that Papa was still alive. You couldn't shake it out of him. Finally, out of sheer exhaustion, Mama conceded that Charlie was right. Papa was still alive. Charlie nearly cracked another rib shouting, "I told you so! I told you so!"

While Charlie was getting over the pain caused by his outburst, Mama had time to think hard about how to handle this one. "Look now, Charlie. You've got something that lots of other people don't have. You've got a special gift of faith. That's what makes you so sure that when people pass away, they don't really pass away. They're still around."

"Ya mean they're right here? Right here in this room?"

"Right here in this very room. Out there on the street, too. You went all over the city trying to find your Papa, and he was with you all the time. He probably worried himself sick, seeing you knocked over by that van."

"Where was he then? I didn't see him. How come he didn't help me out?"

"You didn't die, did you?" Mama snapped.

Charlie nodded soberly.

"Well, isn't that evidence enough?"

"Yeah, but where is he? He wasn't in that box, Mama, I keep telling you that an' nobody believes me."

"You were right, Charlie. It was only a dummy in that box. What you saw was a corpse. It's just like a shell. There isn't anything inside it. Now Papa can go anywhere he wants. He can travel with us, and he won't even get older as time goes on."

"Can I talk to him then?"

"Sure, you can. All you've got to do is talk. He's around

us, all the time, listening."

Charlie drank it all in greedily, and it was just the medicine he needed. He settled down. His eyes got droopy, and Mama tiptoed out. An astute nurse caught her just before she dropped, and she whisked her onto a gurney.

Charlie was stretched out with his head on Mama's lap before the plane took off. We had boarded early and there had been delays. Finally, the engines began to hum and the plane taxied away from the gate. I watched Mama intently from across the aisle. If she had bestowed Papa with a spirit, it was more than she had done for herself. She rustled Charlie from his sleep and told him to put his seatbelt on. Then she looked out the window for a long time. I couldn't see her face from where I sat, but I knew she was crying when the plane lifted off. Charlie watched her too, like an anxious little gnome, and after a moment he did something only Charlie could do. He stuck his hand out against her cheek to catch a tear. It flickered and rolled down his finger like a falling star. Then he clasped his hands together and started to pray.

Mama turned to him and smiled weakly. Charlie just continued on, whispering inaudible words with his eyes pinched shut. As far as I know, Mama never went to church again. But Charlie did.

CHAPTER 8

FAIRY TALES

The years between five and eight were the longest in my childhood. Time dragged, and I lost whatever it is that makes babies irresistible. Thank God that during that period I learned to read. Living in other people's stories brought some of the old sparkle back to life, though it was an existence spent entirely in my head. Mama used to joke that if ever I fell off a cliff it would be for the nose in my book.

Just after I turned seven, a year I drowsily assumed would be as long and routine as the last, a fantasy world opened up to me. The zaniest stories and characters stepped in from out of the blue, filling the corners of my room with a circus tent of invisible delights. The more books I read, the more I imagined, until the real world retreated and fantasy took residence in my mind.

I discarded the plain Alice Montgomery like an old doll. The truth, I convinced myself, was that I was no ordinary mortal at all. I had sailed down to earth in a bubble, along with all my other imagin-lings. I was a fairy spirit in human disguise, a white witch invested with supernatural powers I had yet to discover. Everybody else belonged to the mundane world of cold mashed potatoes and canned peas. Before going to bed at night, I'd stare at my face in the mirror, expecting the image at any moment to dissolve and reveal my true distinctiveness.

In early December, Papa came home one night with big scrolls of paper under his arm. He announced that he had met an old man at lunch who was a friend of the architect who designed our Toronto house back in 1905. Papa took off his suit jacket and unrolled the translucent sheets of paper on the kitchen table. While we crowded around, he studied the thin blue veins running this way and that on the pages, which in no way appeared to resemble our house. Papa reported that the original architect had built nine rooms on the ground floor, which indicated that there was one room we hadn't discovered yet. Well, I can tell you, that piece of news stirred us up like a flock of blackbirds. We jostled to peer at the blueprints as Papa ran his finger along the maze of markings, but the magic lines did not reveal any secrets. Finally, Papa shook his head and pointed to the date on the blueprints – 1926. "They must have renovated," he said, rolling up the paper with the mystery.

Our house had inherited a reputation in the neighborhood for being haunted. As the story goes, the first owner was a woman who shaded all the windows with big striped awnings after her husband died. That much was true. The evidence was still rolled up in the basement cellar. The widow stayed in the darkness alone for some time. Food must have reached her somehow, but the neighbors never saw her come or go. Then one day she hurled herself off the third-floor balcony and fell to her death on the landing below. The boxes in the cellar contained the remains of a couple of families, including a badly painted portrait of a woman who looked like a bulldog wearing a black Edwardian dress. We all figured she was the widow, and everyone accepted the fact that she reigned supreme in the cellar. The basement was the eeriest place in the whole house, and little Charlie and Zack wouldn't venture down there if their lives depended on it. I was afraid of the cellar, too, but the lure of its artifacts overpowered my better instincts. I found dozens of boxes of old photographs and little dolls in Victorian clothing that would tear with the slightest tug. In deference to the widow, I never took anything out of the basement. Neatness may not be in my nature, but everything had to be restored to its rightful place and handled carefully. Like an archeologist I spent hours in the cellar, unearthing the trappings of a bygone age. I was too young to put anything together, but it felt wonderful to handle all the objects and turn over the stones of lives that seemed so much larger than my own.

Papa had inherited our Toronto house from his father. Strictly speaking, he didn't inherit it, he had to buy it from the company after his father's death. Grandfather had made a fortune in real estate, and our old, rambling brick house was one of his earliest acquisitions. Papa had been eying it since childhood. Grandfather might have known the real story behind the widow's death, but if he did, it went to the grave with him. I do remember Papa telling Charlie that he liked old houses because "old walls have good ears." He was headed down the hall carrying Charlie to bed.

"Where are the ears?" Charlie asked. Papa put him down and pointed to the oak wainscotting. "Well, you have to look for the eyes first…. See that knot there? That's an eye."

Charlie touched the knot. "Is it looking at me?" he shrieked.

"Sure it is." Papa could be quite wicked sometimes, although he never meant to be. In any case, Charlie was quite shaken by the idea that walls have eyes and ears. He saw eyes everywhere, and maybe that helps to explain his earnest wish to please God.

The house in Toronto had dozens of little rooms with nooks and crannies that we used to explore. Each one was a miniature universe with its own character. Papa inhabited the office along the main hallway to the living room. It was full of books, magazines, *National Geographics,* and old newspapers that he collected with a fetish and piled in stacks on the floor. Papa had nothing but a few old pairs of trousers when he decided to settle down, but once he took root, he started collecting everything and he might have buried himself in his own paraphernalia if he had let it go on.

Beside Papa's office was a small bar with a scaled-down refrigerator and little cupboards for storing alcohol. "Spirits," he called them. "Best to put the spirits in one room and keep them under lock and key," he would say. The library across from the hall was the focus of all Montgomery family gatherings. It was an intimate room with a blue Persian carpet, a stone fireplace, and oak-paneled walls. Two walls were filled with the over-flow of Papa's books—dusty leather-covered tomes that nobody ever read— but if you pressed one of the oak panels in just the right spot, it opened like a door to a narrow staircase leading upstairs to Mama and Papa's bedroom. They called it their "escape hatch", but for us it was the "secret passage" and, I might add, a real party trick for uninitiated friends.

The idea that there might be a hidden room in the Montgomery house was not so surprising in itself because the house was full of secrets. But a renovation directly after the widow's death in 1926 could only mean one thing to me and Jeffrey—a large-scale cover-up.

We began an investigation that very night after Papa rolled up the blueprints. I started with the least obvious places, looking in closets and peering under stairs. Jeffrey roamed from room to room, methodically taking in the whole picture without touching a thing. He ended up in Papa's office, where he stayed for some time. Then he went outside and, after a few moments, he burst through the front door and headed straight back to the office. He pushed on one of the panels, which we had all done a thousand times. Papa had a door in the wall of his office that was exactly like the one in the library, but it wasn't nearly as interesting because it just opened to more bookshelves. When I entered Papa's office, Jeffrey was hauling the books off the shelves and piling them on Papa's overflowing desk. "The secret room is here," he whispered without looking up. "Outside there's a space between the office and the bar down the hall. And it's right behind this door. C'mon, take a look. These shelves aren't made of oak like the rest. They're made of something else. Maybe pine."

I peered over his shoulder, and sure enough, the wood was different. It looked cheap—stained a dark color—and the shelves were shallow, capable of holding only paperbacks. The board behind them was made of similar stained wood.

My thoughts raced. It was so obvious! Why had no one ever thought to ask if this door in Papa's office was in fact a door? But there it was, a very shabbily disguised door, from my point of view. From the door's point of view, even a shabby disguise served well enough. It performed its function as a bookcase with confidence, knowing that the morons who had bought the house would never discover what it was hiding. I felt convinced that we had found the widow's burial chamber. It seemed perfectly reasonable to me that she would want to be entombed in the house she had already made into a grave with those dreadful awnings.

Now it was only a matter of breaking through that wall. I made the mistake of telling Mama what I surmised we would find behind the false front, and maybe the idea frightened her a little. If it did, she didn't show it, she just patted my head as if I were some kind of domestic pet and called me "Miss Melodrama". She made the point to Papa, however, that she flatly opposed any initiative to open up that wall. Mama was in charge when it came to architectural modifications of our house, and she would not tolerate this infraction.

In the end, however, the majority ruled, and for the sake of peace, Papa came downstairs the next morning followed by a squad of munchkins in sleepers, armed with his tools. He removed the shelves and then prised open the wall. All night I'd been preparing for the worst, and now I could stomach anything. Anything but nothing! Just another brick wall. Rock solid, stubborn red brick. No telling whether it was old brick or new. Just brick. No getting around it. I couldn't have imagined a greater disappointment. Papa seemed enormously pleased. He banged the pine wall back in place and told us the case was closed. I remember thinking, "What's the matter with grown-ups?" If it had been up to me, I would have used dynamite before I'd turn my back on a mystery. Who in their right mind could live with a riddle like that and not be haunted by it, night and day? But Mama and Papa were content to leave it there and carry on with their humdrum lives. "Forget it," they said. "Let's not dwell on it."

"But we're dwelling *in* it!" I insisted. They ignored me. Bizarre.

As Christmas approached, I got it into my head to organize a play. I'd been reading all Andrew Lang's colored fairy books and my mind had started hatching a plot. The boys agreed that if I came up with the story and the costumes, and the parts weren't mushy, they'd go along with it. As Miss Melodrama, I was determined to make a big impression with my theatrical debut.

One Saturday afternoon a few days before Christmas, I was upstairs, dreaming about how to put this together. Mama and Papa had gone to a matinee. It was the first time I recall them ever leaving us alone with Jeffrey in charge. Well, let me tell you, he took his first opportunity for parental authority to heart. He spent the whole time sprawled on his belly in the library, watching TV with the stereo going full blast.

Charlie made a big scene when Mama left. You would think being five would make him old enough to let go of Mama for a couple of hours. But not Charlie. We used to say Charlie was Mama's third foot. When the door closed between him and his Mama, he took it as pure rejection. He stomped around in the foyer for a while and then headed upstairs. Four-year-old Zack was in his bedroom, playing quietly with his train set. Charlie barged in and took over building the track in a big circle on the floor. Zack didn't seem to mind at first. It was in his nature to content himself with his lot when others intruded on his territory. He gathered up the few pieces of track that remained and started putting them together in a line. Once Charlie had finished building his own track, he took hold of the remote control and ran the train around and around. Zack shrieked with delight, so Charlie made it go faster. And faster. And then too fast. Zack whimpered. Charlie knew his baby brother was terrified, but he had a big ball of rage inside and he had to get it out of his system. When the train wouldn't go any faster, Charlie went crazy. Flung the control box into the middle of the circle and grabbed the engine. Spun the train around with his hand until the caboose flew off and hit Zack in the eye.

Zack stood up and wailed at the top of his lungs. I admit I heard him from my perch outside the big oak doors, but I didn't feel like breaking up another stupid fight. When nobody came to his aid, Zack started shrieking, and Charlie put a hand over his mouth to stifle him. Zack struggled and then he bit Charlie's hand. That did it.

Charlie dragged him to the closet, threw him in, and

139

slammed the door. While Zack bawled, Charlie stood there with his foot jammed against the closet door. He told Zack that if he shut up, he'd let him out. Zack must have sobbed for nearly half an hour before he quieted down, and by that time Charlie had purged his demons. He was back to the trains, playing as if he'd forgotten the whole thing. I don't know what poor Zack went through in that closet, but he didn't come out after Charlie said he could. He just stayed there, like he'd come to accept it. Jeffrey ambled in nearly two hours later to check things out. Charlie was sitting on the floor in the midst of an elaborate track.

"Where's Zack?" Jeffrey asked.

"I dunno," Charlie lied. He looked up at Jeffrey and scratched his armpit nervously. "Well I guess he's in the closet, 'cause that's where I put him."

"What?" Jeffrey stamped over to the closet and opened it up. There was Zack, all curled up in a fetal position, staring into the dark with big dilated pupils. Jeffrey picked him up. At first Zack seemed to be in shock, but after a moment he put his arms and legs around Jeffrey's torso like an orphaned monkey and whimpered pathetically. Jeffrey let him down ever so gently onto the bed and headed for Charlie in a rage. Grabbing him by the hair, he nearly shook his head off while Charlie screamed blue murder. "Mama! Mama! I WANT MAMA!" Jeffrey took him by the shirt and was dragging him to the closet to get a taste of his own medicine when Mama walked in. In a split second she sized up the situation, marched directly over to Charlie, gathered him into her arms, and let Jeffrey have it.

"I leave you in charge of these children for three hours and look what happens. I'd like to know what's the matter with you.... You.... You've got a real mean streak in you, mister. I must have been crazy to leave you alone with my children. I don't trust you, Jeffrey Montgomery. And I'm not even sure I *like* you."

Jeffrey gawked at Mama in shock. I'm sure she didn't mean to say what she said, but the words were out. She hugged Charlie tightly. Zack sat up on the bed and leaned against the wall, sucking his knuckles, and staring at the scene in abject bewilderment. Poor Jeffrey felt gut-punched by the injustice. He stalked out of the room saying, "I hate that little bastard Charlie." His voice cracked on the word "hate", and the rest of the words came out so high and thin they could hardly be heard.

After witnessing that scene, I went up to the attic to rummage through some old clothes. Finding a wardrobe for my play was hopeless. What was stored up there was identical to what we had in our drawers, only older. I had three screwball actors to outfit, not including myself. You'd think some merciful ghost would have given me just a bit of a head start for my first performance by providing some workable material. But oh no. And furthermore, I didn't have the faintest idea how to dramatize the fairy tale I had patched together. I didn't know what I was doing, but I *did* know that it had to come out flawlessly, like in the movies. Nobody had ever counselled me on reaching too high. I only did what came naturally, and that was to assume that all my fabulous visions could be brought from heaven to earth as neatly as a peach flambé delivered on a silver platter.

The story took place high on a mountain, nestled in a quiet valley. A witch lived there, who was known throughout the countryside for her good spells. The witch had one knockout of a daughter, and princes for hundreds of miles were clamoring to get a look at her. One day, a handsome prince who lived many miles to the north got wind of this damsel and set off with his companion and an entourage of soldiers. I could easily imagine the spectacle of all those tall young soldiers riding through the lush mountainside with their gilded breastplates flashing in the sun.

The prince's companion was a hunchback who had been with him since childhood. The prince had come to rely on this hunchback because the little man had something the handsome prince could never dream of possessing—charm! Horrible and ugly as he was, the hunchback was so likeable that when the prince went off to a tournament, he would be forced to bring the hunchback along just to ensure a respectable turnout.

When the prince came to the mountain village (cue fanfare), he knocked on the witch's door and her beautiful daughter opened it. She was dazzled by the dashing prince but spooked by his companion. Looking into her eyes with an expression of warm intelligence, the hunchback took the hand of the witch's daughter and instantly subdued her. The prince spoke to her for a few moments, but the girl became so bored that he made an excuse to go and see the horses. Then she had a lovely chat with the hunchback, who proved to be so merry and gentle-hearted that before she knew it, the witch's daughter had fallen in love with the ugly little man. Right in the middle of a very intense moment, the prince strolled in to find the hunchback in the girl's arms. Outraged, he called for his soldier to tie the girl up and kill the hunchback. But this was no ordinary girl. When the prince tied her to the chair, she cast a spell on him, intended to take effect should one arm be raised against the hunchback. The soldier drew his sword to kill the little man, and his arm froze in midair. Both he and the prince were turned to stone. With the prince's transformation, the hunchback began to straighten and grow taller. He threw off his rags, and lo and behold, a full-bodied prince emerged. As he explained, he was the real prince all along, but was taken from his cradle at birth and replaced by a changeling, the son of an evil witch. They embraced, and everyone lived happily ever after.

Jeffrey got to be both prince and narrator. Coming up with the idea of a narrator was a real brainstorm that saved me the fatal effort of having to create a realistic mountain scene. The hunchback's part was demanding, and he had to be an affectionate sort of character, so the obvious choice was Charlie. Zack would have to play the soldier. Not very convincing but, I rationalized, there must have been a couple of dwarfs around in those days who would be tough enough to get into the army. A little makeup and some arm stuffing would make Zack look fierce as a dog.

As for my own part, it was demanding as all get-out. Now I don't want to put anybody down here, least of all myself, but I wasn't exactly a beauty to die for. For starters, I wasn't a blonde. I had huge feet and a face that would have looked more appropriate on the head of an insect. It made me sick, thinking, "How am I going to persuade my audience that I can draw princes for miles without them guffawing?" I had to be beautiful. When it all came down to it, I was the worst material I had.

Not to be defeated, I went downstairs to see what I could find in Mama's old cedar closet. It was a spacious square room that smelled like history. Dresses from her college days hung in garment bags on opposite sides of the room, and cardboard boxes of old clothes were stacked against the third wall. I loved rooting in those old boxes. I wasn't allowed to touch the enclosed dresses, but the boxes were fair game. Right away, I found a pink satin slip that looked as if it might do the trick. I also found a piece of embroidered gauze from an old curtain. I figured I would make a cone out of colored cardboard and attach the gauze at the back for a veil. The rest would have to be pure performance.

I had at least half a dozen tights in a variety of the most revolting earth shades you can imagine, so everybody would be covered from that end up. Mama gave me three of Papa's old shirts for the boys, which we tied with sashes at the waist. That, and a leotard for Zack into which we could pack rags for muscles, completed the costumes. I wrote out a few paragraphs for the narrator to read at the opening of the play. At first, Jeffrey didn't want to rehearse because he was still angry at Charlie, but when I started to cry because he was ruining everything, including Christmas, he thrust out his hand and said, "Fine, give me the script. Let's just get this over with."

I wanted the boys to be natural when they played out their parts, and they had to know the story well enough that we could be reasonably sure nobody would take a wrong turn. It required a few group rehearsals, none of which lasted more than ten minutes, because that was the sum total of their attention spans. During the third rehearsal, I nearly burst a blood vessel out of frustration. These boys were not actors. They had none of the early signs of greatness, no distinctive otherworldly qualities. They were drones, destined to drudgery. Drones, drones, all of them, drones!

I had begun to smell defeat, but I couldn't give up. My entire life depended on creating that little piece of magic on a makeshift stage.

"No, Jeffrey, you can't do it that way. Come in the front door, the way Papa would enter."

Jeffrey stepped out the imaginary door of the witch's house and started the scene again. He knocked on space and sauntered back in with his soldier Zack in tow. He looked around with a silly grin on his face. "You mean I gotta wear tights on my legs, Alice? I'm not gonna wear tights."

"Jeffrey, c'mon. Concentrate! Forget about the tights. You've just walked in on the beautiful witch's daughter. You're supposed to look at me and be breath-taken by my beauty."

Jeffrey broke up. "Oh yeah? Hahaha! What beauty?" He cuffed Zack on the shoulder. "Soldier, do you see any beauty in here?"

"Nope, just a toad!"

Jeffery pushed Zack at me, saying, "See if she'll turn into something. Go on, kiss her. Kiss the toad!"

"No! Ew, ew, yuck!"

I was out of my depth.

"Okay, I'm ready!" Charlie came running into the living room in mud-colored tights that extended well beyond his toes and tripped him up on the carpet. Papa's shirt hung down to his knees.

"Okay, Charlie, let's see your hunchback imitation," I said. Charlie bent over and slapped his hands on his knees. Not bad. I resumed command. "Okay, Charlie, enter with Jeffrey. Soldier, you come in later." Jeffrey rolled his eyes and went through the motions again. "Knock, knock. Hello, lady … I mean, *my* lady." The prince stuck a leg out and bowed stiffly. "Nice day, huh?" Of course, he'd forgotten his lines, but his painful stupidity actually worked.

"What do I do?" Zack asked, getting impatient.

"I'll figure that out in a second. Let's get Charlie going first." Time churned on. After five more minutes of going in and out an imaginary door, Charlie's enthusiasm began to grate. He kept jumping around the prince like some kind of spider monkey. I had to call it quits.

We had four days before Christmas, and during that time I put those poor boys through at least a dozen rehearsals. For me, it was intensely important that the play come off without a hitch. And in spite of the ridiculous nature of the whole thing, every rehearsal did in fact run a little smoother than the last one. I learned, however, that it was easiest to rehearse the boys separately. That way there weren't so many distractions.

Christmas Eve arrived at last. Jeffrey and I hung an old black blanket across half the library to mark off the stage. A couple of old chairs, a table, and a wooden cabinet with a few meagre pots and a loaf of bread furnished the inside of the witch's house. Mama had given us the Christmas tree to portray the out-of-doors. No one was supposed to see the set until the curtain was removed, and it really wasn't such a bad effort for a bunch of amateurs. Before going down the hall and taking my place on set, I had a final look at myself in the mirror on the door of the guest bathroom. I had painted my lips with dark red lipstick and drawn eyelash lines under my eyes. I looked almost exotic. The pink satin slip (stuffed with a couple of socks) gave me an adult woman's body. Gone was the long, lanky, and certainly-not-destined-to-be-cheerleader type, Grade B school kid. I smiled at myself. I could be bewitching. I could be sad. I could be demure. I was an enchantress. "This is going to be my Cinderella night," I told myself. My true, magical nature would become apparent to all.

Showtime. I instructed Mama to turn off the lights in the library, and she (along with Papa and Bel) took their seats in front of the black curtain. Jeffrey sat on a high stool to the right of the curtain and began the narration, while Charlie, crouching on the floor, shone a flashlight on his face. I was amazed at Jeffrey. His narration actually brought some life to the opening of the play, and I was positive that our audience members were impressed. I could have hugged Jeffrey for starting us off right. Then he smoothly pulled the curtain back and tied it on one side. I bent down to turn on the floor light behind the wooden cabinet in the witch's house. There I was, sitting at the table in all my glory, working on a piece of embroidery. After a few moments, I sighed, set it down on the table, got up, and began to pace the room.

"Oh, I do wish that my life could be more interesting. It really is terribly lonely living way up here with only Mama, though she is a good witch, to be sure." I sighed again. "To be sure" was Jeffrey's cue. I sighed again, thinking, "Darn you, Jeffrey. Have you got plans to show up tonight or what?"

I picked up the sewing and took my seat again. Finally, Jeffrey knocked on the imaginary door—Charlie made the sound effect offstage—and he entered with a stiff, unnatural flourish. He took one look at me, snatched my hand, and planted a kiss on it like he had business to do, so let's get the visit over with.

"This is my companion," he said, pulling the hunchback into the room with a rough twist of the forearm. Charlie had been standing by the imaginary door, all hunched over and gawking at me out of his left eye as if I were Helen of Troy. Jeffrey pushed him forward, and he stumbled toward me, overdoing it. He literally drooled and Mama burst out laughing. I leapt up, trying to act horrified at the sight of this disgusting creature, but Charlie made me feel ridiculous. He grinned at me, nodding his head up and down like a moron.

"So...." the prince announced, looking for pockets in his tights and not finding any. His hands floundered in space, fingers flickering behind his back.

How the heck do you respond to "So"? "So, you've come a long way, I understand," I said, moving languidly across the stage and trying to appear as if concealed a burning interest in this strapping princely specimen.

"Yeah, well, we've been on the road for days," said the prince, hunting around for something to do.

"Are you tired? Or hungry, perhaps?" I spun around with the grace of a dancer circling on a note. The prince was drumming a loaf of bread on the side of the cabinet like he was in a rock band. "Naw, think I'll go out and feed the horses." He ambled out. No wonder the witch's daughter fell for the hunchback, I thought. And there he was, squatting in the corner and ogling me with an expression that hadn't changed since he first came in.

I went and sat at the kitchen table with my back turned to him. He limped over and sat on the floor beside me. Nice effect, Charlie.

"You are a very beautiful witch," he said coyly, scratching his head.

"Thank you, dear little man. You are so kind."

"If I didn't have this awful hump on my back, I'd marry you myself. Do you think your mother could work a spell?"

Why Charlie said that, I don't know. We'd never rehearsed it that way.

"She doesn't really deal in backs," I said, a bit too crisply. I sighed uneasily. I didn't have a line.

"It doesn't matter anyway. I'm happy with my life," said the hunchback. "Are you?"

Now I was prepared for that question at least. "I'm lonely living here all by myself. I'm so far away from everyone, you see." I rested my cheek on my right hand and sobbed a few tears.

"Don't cry," said the hunchback. He stood up and put a hand on my shoulder.

"You are sweeter than anyone I know," I said, covering his hand with my own.

"And you are the most beautiful witch in all the world. I've met many girls at the curt, and you are the nicest of them all." I wished I hadn't asked him to say *court*. It was a word that held no meaning for him whatsoever.

"Well, I expect I'll be betrothed to your master," I said.

The hunchback hobbled off according to plan and put his hand over his eyes, rather too much like a sailor sighting land. "If you choose…."

"If I could choose, dear little man, I would choose you," I said. I rose and went over to him, knelt beside him, and put my arms around his neck. Enter the prince, on cue, with his soldier Zack in tow.

"What's this?" he roared. "My hunchback dares to embrace the woman I mean to take?"

"You mean to take?" I cried. "You haven't even asked me to marry you! And besides, I won't. I've fallen in love with your hunchback."

"Why, you ugly little creep!" Jeffrey lunged at Charlie while Zack grabbed me and dragged me to the chair where he wrapped me in rope.

Then something altogether unanticipated happened. Jeffrey took the hunchback by the throat and started to choke him. Everyone thought it was part of the act until Charlie's face flushed purple and his eyes popped. He tried to scream, but he couldn't because Jeffrey's grip was too tight. Meanwhile I sat tied up in the chair, trying to figure out a way to end the story happily without destroying the illusion. Jeffrey wrestled Charlie to the floor. Zack went up to him and kicked him in the side, while Jeffrey pounded his head on the floor. Suddenly, Jeffrey let him go. Charlie writhed and gasped for breath, and then he started to bawl. Jeffrey knelt over him, his whole body shaking with fury. And fear. I don't think he meant to hurt Charlie as much as he did, but when he got into it, he couldn't stop. Probably the first time he realized the implications of that instinct. Mama was on the stage in a flash. She picked Charlie up and carried him out of the room. Zack scrambled over to Papa like a little chimp, seeking protection.

I remember how Papa sat there motionless while Zack clambered up on his lap. I remember how he sat in the dark, smoking his pipe, as if he were miles away. Sat there and didn't react, calm as the eye of the storm. I remember the hurt I felt in the stage light, tied to the chair in that silly pink slip. There would be no transformation.

I realize now that the true prince, the silent object of all my efforts, was out there sitting in the shadows. Had he acknowledged the meaning of the play, had he smiled, or taken me in his arms, or responded in any way at all, I would have felt special at a time when the world was starting to grow very large and I was growing very small.

The vision I have of Papa sitting in the dark and drawing on his pipe was the first thought, the formative one, the one that began this long story. It's a memory I can't erase. I don't know what has kept it breathing all these years. It's a memory that has no meaning in itself. It can only engender other memories. And all the other memories, all the other stories are just false fronts for the central one, which may be the real one, I don't know. I only know that when you start prying walls open to reveal secrets, when you really think you're close to the answer, you're likely to run into brick. There's no getting around it. The real story is always buried. Or maybe it's not there at all.

CHAPTER 9

A RATTLE
OF BONES

A unt Bel died a few months ago, in August 1980. It was quite sudden. She had a fast-moving liver cancer. Mama visited her in hospital only once before her speedy exit from the world. We all went to the funeral, including the mysterious Ro, a well-coiffed gentleman in a charcoal grey suit. He had a magnetic presence and smelled like he'd been sitting by a fire that burned maple wood. He made a point of approaching each of us and saying, in soft tones, "I am really so very sorry for your loss."

We all said, "Thank you." *Thank you.* It's such an awkward thing for a grieving family to say, but then, what is natural about a funeral? Nobody engaged with Ro, although I wanted to. I hoped to find an opportunity to speak to him after the service, but by then he had slipped away.

Mama did not seem shaken by the loss of her sister. On the contrary, she seemed alarmingly high-spirited. Had she been drinking? Standing over the closed casket, she gave a short eulogy that began, "As all of you know, Bel and I weren't exactly on the same page. In fact, I have to say that the further away she moved from me, the more affection I felt for her."

Mama wore a black pencil skirt under a grey smock with a white bow. I don't know what possessed her to present herself as a caricature. She went on to share something very personal about Bel, something that few people knew. It was common knowledge that Bel's mother had been institutionalized after contracting "the sleepy sickness". We had all read about the strange epidemic that swept the world after the First World War and put at least a million people to sleep. "But Bel wasn't the type of person who would talk about the traumas of her early childhood," said Mama. "Once, though, she gave me a few details because I was seven, the same age she had been when it happened. She swore me to secrecy but now...." Mama stepped off the dais and placed her hand on Bel's coffin. "I'm sure she won't mind me sharing it. Bel told me that she had gone into her mother's room to say good night. Her mother was sitting in front of the mirror and brushing her long, dark hair. She had frozen in that position. Bel kissed her, and she came to life, but she had a strange look in her eye. Bel said the expression was very keen, like the look of a hawk. Her mother told her to be a good girl, not a nasty one. 'Don't turn into your father,' she said. Little Isabel was unsettled by that, as you might imagine. Then her mother turned to the mirror and stared at herself in a trance. Bel shook her and screamed at her to snap out of it. Her drunken father came into the room and when he saw his wife's condition, he thought she had fallen under an evil spell. He had a lot of old ideas, hangovers, you might say, from his upbringing in Romania. He thought Isabel had inherited his grandmother's dark powers. People said she could poison people's blood or turn them into stone. Being a little girl, Isabel was convinced that she had done it, that she had turned her mother into stone."

Mama's speech was followed by a ripple of gasps. I glanced at Charlie who was sitting next to me. He was clutching his left hand as if he were trying to keep his shock from flying out of his body. His cheeks were highly flushed and he was wearing an ill-fitting beige suit. I don't know what possessed him to wear leopard-patterned socks. Maybe he wanted the comforting reminder of animals when he looked at his feet. Charlie is a country veterinarian living in Okotoks with a house full of parakeets and cats. He's not married, and even now the mention of sex embarrasses him. Jeffrey used to say, "All Charlie needs is a good lay," and there's probably some truth to that. Charlie's a good sort, though. He visits me from time to time, and on every occasion brings along a different inhabitant of the animal kingdom.

Last month it was a racoon. A few weeks before that, he produced a coyote pup that was born on the Sarcee Reserve. Unfortunately it died several days later.

Charlie caught my eye, and we breathed a big sigh together. I noted the deep line between his tearing eyes. He seemed to be experiencing a sudden spring of compassion for Bel. He had helped her out, right to the end of her life. I don't know if he ever got the blessing he sought, but those tears spilling from his eyes made me wonder if it wasn't happening, right there and then.

After the service, I stood outside the church with my brothers who were all looking for ways to escape. Most of the other people there had known Bel through her work in schools and libraries. They spoke about her "big personality" and her "colorful character".

Mama made the rounds, greeting people graciously. She wore her social smile, the only smile we see nowadays. It's warm, but formal. It says, "I'm happy to see you, but keep your distance." If you phone her just to chat, she will remind you that she has a lot on her plate. She's got her students, her gallery, and the demands of her own work. She lives in Mount Royal, teaches at the college, and surrounds herself with protégés who vie to become her private students. This year she handpicked five aspiring artists who get regular instruction and a place to exhibit and sell their work. In turn, she requires each of them to supervise the gallery on the ground floor one day a week.

The truth is, Mama has managed to clutter up her life with so much activity that her own kids feel like exiles, reminders of a period ridden with turmoil that is now, mercifully, over and forgotten. I try to deny it, but I think Mama prefers her art to our company, perhaps because in the end it is more controllable. It may reveal her, but it doesn't harbor resentment or stick her with accusations.

Jeffrey couldn't wait to leave the memorial. He stood outside the funeral home, inching his way toward the parking lot. Any moment he would bolt. His hands were thrust into the pockets of a blue fleece jacket. It wasn't appropriate for the occasion, unless we were cross-country skiing to the service. I strode over to talk to him. "Hey, before you escape, Jeffrey, at least tell me what you're up to now that you're a fully certified electrical engineer."

He glanced past me, catching the eye of a pretty girl with long dark hair who wore knee socks and saddle shoes and could not have been more than sixteen. Jeffrey and his damn good looks. Always looking, always watched, ever the possible tryst.

"I'm going to Paris," he said.

"Oh, yeah?" Charlie approached. He was already removing his jacket and yanking out his shirt tails.

"Yup, that's the plan," said Jeffrey. "You going to complete that striptease, Charlie? I know a burlesque theatre that is looking for a man just like you."

"What are you gonna do in Paris?" Charlie asked, ignoring the joke.

"Pick up some French." Jeffrey grinned. "I intend to become quite fluent."

"Let's just hope you don't pick up anything else," I remarked.

Then Zack approached. He'd already doffed his grey suit jacket, and he looked thin as a rail in a white T-shirt and jeans. "When is this thing going to be over?" he asked. He checked his watch. We all gaped at its big round clock face, wondering how Zack could afford that treasure while paying his medical school tuition. He raked his fingers through his cropped dark hair. "I gotta get back to the hospital," he said. "See ya."

I trailed him into the parking lot. "Hey, Zack?"

"Yeah, what's up?"

I wanted to hug him. When he was little, we had a close bond. A river of time roared between us, but some rebel spirit in me wanted to make a bridge. "I've always had this question, Zack. Did Mama ever give you any details about Papa's death?"

"Nope, but I intend to get them from her," he said, opening the trunk of his yellow Nissan. He stuck his jacket through a garment bag, slid it onto a hanger, and laid the bag flat.

"Really? You think you can?"

"She owes me." He zipped up the garment bag and slammed the trunk. "Sorry Alice, gotta go."

I wandered back into the empty church and sat in a pew. I sat there for the longest time, staring at Bel's coffin.

It was the end of August, but I couldn't get warm, even in the heat, even in a pink crocheted sweater and a grey wool dress.

Nearly a year passed. May came around. I had stopped writing family stories. The ones I had already written sat in a file folder on my desk, but I swear those pages didn't rest. They fluttered anxiously. Images followed me, interjecting themselves into other streams of thought.

I told myself I should never have pursued those childhood memories because once I had found them, I couldn't seem to create a fiction that would put Papa to rest. That formative vision of him smoking in the dark after the theatrical debacle stayed with me like a dream I couldn't shake. Dreams dissolve, but not apparitions. Papa's ghost inhabited me, unappeased. What I had blundered into or why, I didn't understand. He was still there looking out of the darkness, saying nothing, sitting there in that painful stillness, while all around him memories with no meaning flew up in a circular wind. I tried to pull them down, anchor them, but I couldn't. I couldn't make sense of anything.

I had nearly finished my PhD dissertation in history, and I felt relieved that I didn't have to do any more research. I didn't have to try to understand anything, and that made it possible to function. I think I was becoming allergic to the past, especially my own, because whenever

I thought about it, my heart started thumping furiously. I couldn't breathe. I had horrible spells where I felt like I was going to suffocate, and then suddenly they would be over. I would be able to draw air again. I would be released.

The only explanation I dared to give this state of affairs was that Papa had taken up residence in me; that he believed—or perhaps knew—that I could release him. But how? What did he want from me?

I decided that I needed to call Zack. I had been avoiding it. My family made it very easy to avoid contact, but if Zack had learned the facts of my father's death, I needed to know them.

He sounded sleepy when I called. "Yes?"

"It's me, Zack. Alice. Did I wake you?"

"Yeah. It's okay. What time is it? Oh Jesus, I'm late. What's up?"

"I was wondering if you'd talked with Mama. Have you found out anything? If it's not a good time.… "

"Uh, well, yes. But no, it's not a good time, Alice."

I suggested dinner at a Greek restaurant near the hospital, and he was game, so we set a date on the weekend.

Zack had mentioned the restaurant before. It was one of his favorite "haunts", as he put it. The downstairs floor of an old house on 16th Avenue had been made into an intimate, candlelit space with blue and white checkered tablecloths. We met in the foyer, and on the way to the table, Zack stopped at the bar and ordered a carafe of retsina, a Greek wine that I hadn't tasted before. He handed me a menu, and we ordered from the bar. Moussaka for him, a Mediterranean plate for me. Typical Zack, never one to waste time. Efficient.

The bartender brought the carafe to the table and poured the wine into small glasses. It was sharp and bitter—not my cup of tea. "It tastes like it's been stored in a tree for a thousand years," I remarked.

"That's pretty accurate. It's made with pine resin." He swirled the contents of his glass. "I love this stuff. The Romans used to seal it in pine caskets."

My heart skipped several beats. "Caskets?"

He grinned. "Amphorae, actually."

"Right." I changed the subject and asked him questions about his residency. He told me about the ungodly hours and squash games with a wealthy older man, a neurosurgeon.

The conversation lapsed. We weren't here to talk about his relationships or where he got that gold watch, much as I wanted to know. It was time to get to the point. "So, when did you see Mama?"

"Couple of months ago."

He stretched his neck on both sides like he was loosening up to go into the ring.

"Did Mama give you details about the way Papa died?"

"Yep." The candle flame flashed in his smoky green eyes. "They found him in a vault, Alice. The bank had closed. Everyone had gone home. He shot himself in the head. One bullet through the mouth directed at the base of the brain. Very clean."

I concentrated on breathing, slowly, evenly. The meal arrived.

"You wanted the facts," he said, drawing his plate close.

The smell of lamb turned my stomach. "What did he use?"

"A Colt semi-automatic. The only thing his father ever gave him, apparently."

A ball of tears grew in my throat. I couldn't show them. Not to Zack. "But why? Why did he do that?"

"I don't know. Go write some more fiction, Alice. That's your only hope of getting an answer to that question." He dove into his moussaka.

He seemed to have no feelings whatsoever about Papa's death. Why did he even want to know the facts in the first place? I knew the answer to that. Zack was tidy. He would want to establish them, label them like a specimen, and store them away. I noted how his cheekbones had sharpened over the years. His hair was spiked, his suits were always pressed, and he had no flesh on his bones. He was as clean and clinical as an uncovered bulb.

It wasn't entirely surprising to me that my father committed suicide, but up until then I had not been able to admit the possibility. The amount of reorganizing required to make that one fact welcome was exhausting even to consider. I had a beautiful picture of Mama at the center of my fiction, and I had staved off unwelcome facts with the ferocity of her lizzies. In return, she had given me what?

The breathlessness came back. I got up. "Sorry, Zack, but I'm not feeling well. I need some air."

"You should go home and rest," he said.

I took his advice and left him sitting at the table, calmly and methodically dissecting his meal.

I hoped that knowing the facts would silence Papa's ghost, but he remained inside me. Writing stories could take me no farther. Only my feet, it seemed, could do that. I walked a great deal, up and down the river, over bridges, desperate for oxygen and release. My doctor recommended a vacation. I suppose she thought ghosts didn't go on vacation. She considered sending me to a psychiatrist, but I resisted. I wasn't suffering from an abnormality of the mind. I was occupied by a ghost. How do you get rid of a ghost?

And did I want to? Papa's ghost had settled fondly in me. His personality grew warmer and more loving by the day. I found comfort in the thought that my physical ailments were part and parcel of the problem of accommodating two beings in one body. It was hard on us both. If only I knew how to appease us.

A few months later, I went to visit Mama. I did not choose to go. I went to see her because I had received a telegram from Jeffrey, announcing that he was going to be married in Marseilles, the home of his fiancée. What they would do for a living, he didn't have the space to say. I called the gallery first, knowing that Mama would probably resent an unannounced appearance. On the way over, I was overcome by another one of my spells. I went into a cold sweat and nearly side-swiped a bus. The July heat was suffocating, even with all the windows down, but the near accident startled me to my senses. By the time I pulled into the long driveway leading to Mama's residence, I had regained a degree of composure.

The door jangled chimes when I opened it and entered the foyer. There was no one about, so I went through the arched entrance of the gallery and dallied there for a few moments. It was a stately room with a high slanted ceiling, a skylight and a large picture window facing the back garden. Huge dahlia and rose blossoms were bobbing gayly through the glass. Mama had modernized the old house to create her gallery. She lived upstairs on the second and third floors.

The walls, painted a soft yellow, displayed a few watercolors. One in particular attracted my attention. It was clearly Mama's work—a simple picture of a potted orchid set in front of a window with four panes. One tendril seemed to be struggling to reach an elusive shaft of light, a ray so pale and delicate that it seemed the shoot would never thrive. It gave me the feeling that the light had fled, leaving nothing but a trace of warmth.

The plant had a happy spirit, but it wasn't flourishing for all its effort. I noticed the outline of a cat through one of the panes, a muddy shadow moving down the street. You had to show interest in the picture to see the cat, something very much in the style of Madeline Duval.

"Is that you, Alice?" she called from upstairs. "C'mon up. I'm making tea." I went around to the hallway and climbed the long staircase. Mama was pouring steaming water into the pot, while a young woman in her early twenties was putting cups and spoons in saucers. Three sets, I noted irritably. I shouldn't have hoped for the chance of speaking to Mama alone.

"We haven't seen you for a while, Alice. You must be getting near the end of that thesis. How's it going?"

She brought the pot to the table and sat down, while her student hovered about, pouring cream into the pitcher and arranging biscuits on a blue pottery plate.

Mama brushed a stray wisp of hair off her forehead and tucked it neatly into a long blue and white printed scarf that she had wrapped around her head and knotted on one side. She had a fondness for Indian cottons, and her loose skirt was printed with the same crisp flowery pattern as the scarf. Her white blouse was open from the neck to the breast; her cleavage partially disguised by silver chains in a variety of lengths. Mama had aged gracefully. Her green eyes were warmer now, winged with pretty little lines, and she still had the wide, fresh smile of a young girl. Only her cheeks betrayed the relentless effects of time. Their color had paled and they had begun to slide, pulling away from her eyes. It gave her face a serious if not a sad appearance, periodically interrupted by not-entirely-effortless bursts of sunshine and smiles.

I wished with all my heart that the student would go away, but she pulled up a third chair and sat down.

"This is Marie Deschamps, Alice. One of my new artists. You'll have to take a look at her work before you leave. Marie's from Montreal. She spent two years at the Banff School, and her work is now in three galleries across the country. That's not bad for twenty-two."

I wondered how long this resume would go on. Marie, a brunette with a bob, bangs, and China doll features, flushed and smiled sweetly at her mentor. I responded with one of those close-lipped smiles that freeze on your face until the corners of your mouth start twitching uncontrollably. I had the horrible feeling that this would go on all afternoon. The air in the kitchen felt too close. There was no breeze coming through the open window overlooking the garden.

Mama and Marie carried the conversation off into a discussion about the relative merits of realism and surrealism, or interpretive realism, or whatever. Marie was arguing that you ought to paint what sells, and realism sells in the west. Presumably she was one of those landscape or animal painters that everyone out here buys. I counted the measures of my breath.

"That's your only problem," Mama said, throwing her

legs apart and clasping her hands between them. "You paint photographs, albeit good ones, and sure people will buy them. But where is the artist? Where are *you* in your pictures? I keep asking you that, and I'm still waiting for answers."

Marie bit down on her biscuit sullenly and finished her tea in silence. She was a striking girl with heavy eyebrows that pointed downward ponderously as if they belonged to some antiquated scholar or theologian.

Mama looked at me and returned my frozen, flinching smile. "We're boring Alice to tears. You two should get to know one another, you'd probably hit it off. Alice is finishing her PhD in the history of western religions. More tea, Alice?" She offered the pot.

I dove into my purse for refuge. "Mama, I've got a telegram here from Jeffrey that I'd like to discuss with you."

She frowned, still holding the pot. "Is there a problem?"

"No, not a problem. He's going to be married. In Marseilles. He didn't say much more."

"How lovely," Marie exclaimed.

Mama set the pot down abruptly. "No 'I hope you're well, go to hell'?"

"No."

"Did he ask about anyone?"

"No."

"Did he even sign it, 'Love, Jeffrey'?"

"Here, take a look."

Mama unfolded the telegram. It was only one line. It said: "Jeffrey Montgomery and Françoise Lambert will marry September 30 STOP 4 pm Saint-Vincent-de-Paul STOP Jeffrey STOP."

"Figures." She thrust it back at me. The telegram irritated her.

"Can't we discuss this in private?" I snapped. I didn't mean to be offensive, but the tone of my voice grated, even to my own ears. Marie took her half-eaten cookie and fled, visibly hurt.

Mama glared at me. "There was no need to be rude."

"Why can't I ever talk to you alone? You've always got somebody standing guard. It's like you plan it that way."

"That's ridiculous. I've got five students working here, and they've got a free rein to come into the kitchen whenever they wish."

"But what about your family? Your children may desire an occasion to come and talk with you in private."

"I suppose you think Jeffrey wants to talk with me in private? Or Zack?"

"I'm talking about me," I said. "Don't be so defensive."

She got up and poured more water in the kettle. "Alice, I don't want to hurt your feelings, but let's be honest here. You kids don't seem capable of keeping your stones in your pocket when you do visit. I don't know what I've done, but all I feel from the lot of you is resentment. Makes it pretty difficult to let my defenses down." She plugged in the kettle. "Why don't we talk about something else."

"Oh, yeah." I heard my voice crack. With all the turmoil surfacing, I couldn't breathe. I had started to panic. Was I going insane? I was desperately trying to reach her, but Mama wanted to talk about "something else".

"Well, then…." I tugged the elastic out of my hair and shook it out. "What shall we talk about? The arms race? The greenhouse effect? Greenpeace? The green grass? What would go down better with jasmine tea?"

Mama kept her back to me, rattling cups and spoons on the counter.

"Or I suppose we could just sit here together and endure the obligation of a mother-daughter visit by staring into our teacups and talking about, well, let's see … the sale at Woodward's on snow boots or the new fall line at Simpsons…. It's all crap, Mama." I was gasping now, struggling for breath.

"I'm just about ready to show you the door, Alice. Don't push your luck."

"Oh, no, I wouldn't want to do that. Zack tried to do that, and we all know the price he paid for it." Why couldn't I breathe?

Mama spun around. "You don't know the story at all. Zack comes in here shouting obscenities and starts threatening me with his fists. What kind of son is that? He's known about his beginnings for years. I had nothing to do with it. So why does he attack me? I did the best

I could, and I won't stand another tribunal." She defied me with a cold glare.

"I'm not attacking, Mama," I gasped.

"You probably know your father shot himself, but I can't—I *won't* account for it!" She pulled her scarf off her head and hurled it onto the floor. Leaning on the counter, she faced me and rubbed her forehead with a worn hand.

"For years I've been trying to understand why he did it, find ways to explain it … figure out what I did, what weapon in my character drove him to put a bullet through his brain. Your Aunt Bel had me convinced it was all my fault, to say nothing of what she must have said to you kids." The whites of her eyes melted, and two streams of tears ran down her sad slumping cheeks as if there were no end to the ice that had gathered there over the ages.

"I never meant to hurt him, oh God, I never meant to drive him to kill himself…. He killed *himself,* don't you understand?"

"You don't have to tell me all this, Mama." I went to her, put my hand on her shoulder. The open window gave us some air. She shook me away.

"He was so afraid that I would leave him. From the day he met me, he was sure that I would leave him. Why would I leave him? But there was no way to assure him, nothing was good enough and then, in the end, he left me! He left me for another woman, and then he shot himself and left me again!"

Wailing, she slid down the refrigerator and sank into a heap on the floor. She dragged some memos down with her that had been stuck to the fridge with magnets, and I thought about those strips of wallpaper that she'd ripped from the ceiling when she'd had that breakdown after Papa's death. "I thought it was over years ago, I thought I had purged it. But you bring it back, every one of you, as if he were avenging himself on me. You've all turned me into his murderer! Why do you do this to me?" She was shrieking, grabbing the back of her head with both hands as if she were a child trying to shield herself from rifle fire.

Just then, an enormous, pulsing force burst from my ribcage and into my brain. I drew in a deep, deep breath of fragrant, fresh air. Oxygen filled my lungs, filled my cells, expanded my center of being as if I had inhaled the potion that Alice drank. I backed away from the counter and rose higher and higher into the air, weightless. I could see Mama a long way down, shrinking in size, pressed into the underside of the fridge. I had no fear. Slowly, I floated down, featherlike, and reached for her. My fingers touched her shoulders, arms to arms, body to body. I could feel her relax as she absorbed the light that permeated me. I cradled her in my arms and rocked her back and forth. Back and forth.

"Forgive me, Madeline."

Mama blinked hard and stared at me with panic in her eyes. I heard the voice too, resonant and coming from that place at the center of my chest. "I adore you, but I have to leave now. I have to leave again...."

She fingered my lips with a child's wonder, face covered in a tangle of hair. The star burst in my rib cage and rolled away on a long rumble of thunder. Pins of ice shot through my flesh, and for a moment I went completely blind, and colder than I have ever been in my life, dying in a starless void. She clawed her way up the refrigerator, reaching beyond me into the space where he had gone. "Jon! Jon, wait...."

"Bring a blanket, Mama. Hurry!" I cried, feeling my skeleton rattle as if the very marrow had frozen.

Mama ran pell-mell from the room and came back with a quilt. She wrapped it around me, hugged me to her breast, and rubbed my spine furiously with her two palms. The friction kindled some warmth, and slowly my body relaxed as the shivers subsided, one after the other.

"He's been in me for months, Mama, maybe years.... I thought I was going insane." I had to speak, but my teeth chattered, my body felt limp and weak. "I found him, or maybe he found me, I don't know. I didn't know what he wanted.... Oh, God, Mama, all this time it was *you* he wanted to reach!"

She held me tightly in her arms. Her tears felt like rain pattering down my body, washing his fond image away in little rivers as the wind stilled. I tumbled down, down into a blanket of snow, adrift in a forest of pines whispering, "Hush, hush, he's gone now, rest my darling child.... He's gone."

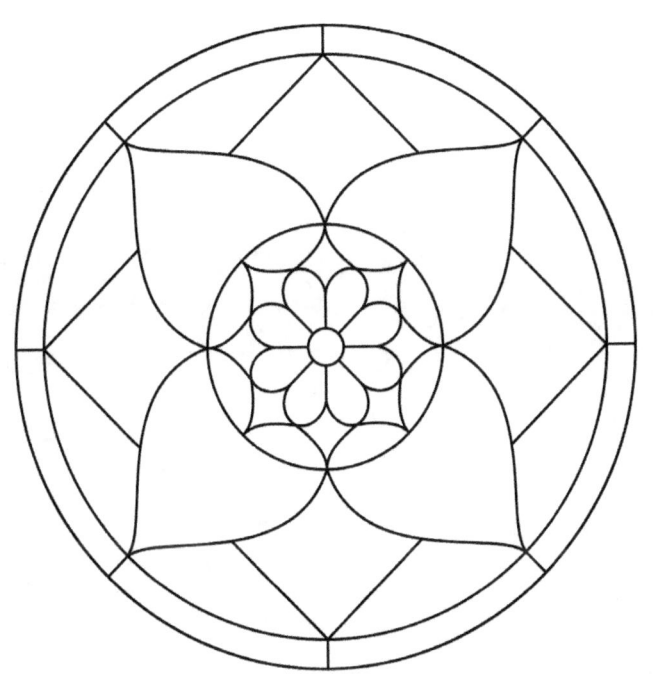

Acknowledgments

I wrote *Outside the Big Oak Doors* when I was in my mid twenties and I had left my home in western Canada to do graduate work in Ontario. I set off with Alice, having no idea where her story would land. All I knew was that she had a powerful wish to bring something out of silence. Decades later, I retrieved the old manuscript from a box in the basement and started reading the story without remembering the ending. It rattled me again, and I marveled that Alice had waited so patiently in a box for so long.

Many thanks to my editor, Diane Young, who has been an enthusiastic champion for Alice and has helped me to open windows in Alice's memory without losing her strong narrative voice. Designer Jennifer Stimson has once again brought her artistry to the book cover and interior design, and I am grateful to Philippa Thompson for her proofreading skills. I should also say that I'm indebted to my family members who have unwittingly inspired some of the scenes in the story, though I hasten to say that all of the characters are purely fictional and not meant to resemble any particular person I have known.

And finally, thanks to my partner, Ian Jaffray, who has heard the entire book read to him in evening episodes that have lit our winter nights with laughter and lively conversation.

ABOUT THE AUTHOR

Michelle Tocher is author of the memoir, *The Tower Princess: A Fairy Tale Lived,* and *How to Ride a Dragon: Women with Breast Cancer Tell Their Stories.* Her works of fiction include *The May Queen, A. Seeker's Storybook,* and most recently, *The Departure Train,* a play about the experience of a woman who boards a train in the afterlife.

Michelle's other lifelong project is wonderlit.com, a website that encourages writers and storytellers to explore wonder tales as way to inspire deep reflection and generate resonant stories for the times.

For more information, visit:

www.michelletocher.com
www.wonderlit.com
www.thedeparturetrain.com